"SASHA WHITE STRETCHE[...]
TO PLACES THIS READER CA[...]
—*Love's Romance*

PRAISE FOR THE NOVELS OF SASHA WHITE

"The writing is strong, the characterization is well drawn and likeable . . . and the sex is very well-done. This is *hot*!"
—Angela Knight, author of the Megaverse series

"Plenty of fun . . . mixes tense emotions and hot sex."
—*Romantic Times*

"Packs a tremendous punch . . . stimulating, steamy, [and] scorching hot."
—*Fallen Angel Reviews*

"Delightful and very thought-provoking."
—*Enchanted in Romance*

"Hot, fast-paced, and erotic."
—*Romance Divas*

"Romance at its best!"
—*Cupid's Library Reviews*

"Hot and explosive."
—*Just Erotic Romance Reviews*

"Intensely sensual."
—*Romance Junkies*

"Creates a carnal haze that envelops the readers, caresses their senses . . . deliciously decadent."
—*The Romance Studio*

"Soul-grabbing, richly evocative, and unforgettable."
—Suzanne McMinn, author of the PAX League series

"Sexy, raw, and intriguing."
—*The Road to Romance*

Berkley Heat titles by Sasha White

BOUND
TROUBLE

Anthologies
KINK

TROUBLE

SASHA WHITE

HEAT
NEW YORK, NEW YORK

THE BERKLEY PUBLISHING GROUP
Published by the Penguin Group
Penguin Group (USA) Inc.
375 Hudson Street, New York, New York 10014, USA
Penguin Group (Canada), 90 Eglinton Avenue East, Suite 700, Toronto, Ontario M4P 2Y3, Canada
(a division of Pearson Penguin Canada Inc.)
Penguin Books Ltd., 80 Strand, London WC2R 0RL, England
Penguin Group Ireland, 25 St. Stephen's Green, Dublin 2, Ireland (a division of Penguin Books Ltd.)
Penguin Group (Australia), 250 Camberwell Road, Camberwell, Victoria 3124, Australia
(a division of Pearson Australia Group Pty. Ltd.)
Penguin Books India Pvt. Ltd., 11 Community Centre, Panchsheel Park, New Delhi—110 017, India
Penguin Group (NZ), 67 Apollo Drive, Rosedale, North Shore 0745, Auckland, New Zealand
(a division of Pearson New Zealand Ltd.)
Penguin Books (South Africa) (Pty.) Ltd., 24 Sturdee Avenue, Rosebank, Johannesburg 2196, South
Africa

Penguin Books Ltd., Registered Offices: 80 Strand, London WC2R 0RL, England

This is an original publication of The Berkley Publishing Group.

This is a work of fiction. Names, characters, places, and incidents either are the product of the author's imagination or are used fictitiously, and any resemblance to actual persons, living or dead, business establishments, events, or locales is entirely coincidental. The publisher does not have any control over and does not assume any responsibility for author or third-party websites or their content.

Copyright © 2007 by Sabrina Ingram.
Cover photo by Lisa Spindler Photography Inc./Veer.
Cover design by Lesley Worrell.
Text design by Tiffany Estreicher.

First edition: August 2007

Library of Congress Cataloging-in-Publication Data

White, Sasha, 1969–
   Trouble/Sasha White.—1st ed.
      p. cm.
   ISBN: 978-0-425-21700-9
   I. Title.
   PS3623.H57885T76 2007
   813'.6—dc22   2007012750

PRINTED IN THE UNITED STATES OF AMERICA

10   9   8   7   6   5   4   3   2   1

TROUBLE

1

It was easy for Samair Jones to stride past the crowd lined up outside the nightclub Risqué and through its front entrance. All it took was a sultry smile for the doorman and she was in.

Okay, so it was more than just the smile. It was the attitude behind the smile. And the happenings of the past few hours had given her just the kick in the ass she needed for an attitude adjustment.

For the past three years she'd been a good girl. She'd worked a "proper" job, had a "proper" relationship, and had a boring, uneventful life. Now it was time to remember how to *live*.

Samair knew there were times when the image she showed

to the world shifted and a certain energy emanated from her that made people sit up and take notice. It was something she used to hate.

The energy was from deep within, and one she hadn't felt in way too long. It was the same energy that had made teachers single her out as the troublemaker in school, and had made her parents berate her for being too flamboyant. But tonight she'd decided to give it free rein.

To give *herself* free rein.

She looked out over the dimly lit dance floor. Friday night and the place was packed and the music was pumpin'. Bodies of all shapes, sizes, and sexes filled the club in varied levels of dress—or, in some cases, undress—undulating to the music. An almost forgotten spark of energy flowed through her. Risqué had a reputation as the classiest dance club in the city, and she could see why. The place was perfect.

Tension eased from between her shoulders as the steady throb of a heavy bass beat seeped into her through the floor, her pulse starting to pound in time with it. She turned from the railing and started for the stairs. Three steps from the top she spotted a good-looking stud on his way up. She smiled at him, held his heated gaze as they passed, and felt the thrill of the hunt shoot through her.

The time had come to stop kidding herself and embrace who, and what, people always told her she was.

Trouble.

*   *   *

Valentine Ward noticed her as soon as she set foot in Risqué. From the vantage point behind the one-way-mirrored wall of his office, he could see everything that happened on the floor of his club. He liked it that way. He needed to know what was happening at all times.

He studied the contradiction of the pretty blonde. The sinuous way she moved had caught his attention. But the longer he gazed at her, the more a subtle air of innocence seemed to come through. "Val, are you listening?"

"Not really," he murmured.

Karl Dawson came up behind him and looked over his shoulder. "Ah, now I see why. A playmate of yours?"

Val watched as she stepped to the side of the landing and surveyed the club from the top floor. She was less than fifteen feet from his office, so he got a good look at her.

Dressed in black slacks and a simple white blouse, she should've looked out of place in the nightclub. The clothes certainly weren't anywhere near the type of party clothes most club-goers wore. They did nothing to hide nor accentuate her curvy figure, and he wondered if she always dressed like that. It looked wrong. Too plain . . . too strict for the raw sensuality she exuded.

Tousled dark blond hair that reached a couple of inches past her shoulders framed a face that housed delicately arched eyebrows, a straight nose, and sensuous lips. The lips were really something. Full and shiny, they formed a natural pout that gave him the urge to suck the bottom one into his mouth for a quick nibble.

He couldn't help but stare, wishing she would look his way. He wanted to see her eyes. Instinct told him they held the key to her.

Val watched those tempting lips tilt in a predatory smile as she started for the steps, and he felt the long-forgotten pull of lust stir.

"Not yet," he finally answered Karl. "But she will be."

Bodies brushed against her as she walked, and Samair felt alive for the first time in way too long. Almost as if she were waking from a deep sleep.

She watched the couple behind the bar as they mixed drinks for the crowd. The male bartender was tall, slim, and clean cut, while the girl was the complete opposite with vivid purple streaks throughout her black hair, heavy eye makeup, and black lipstick. Despite being the odd couple, it was clear they got along as they moved in a synchronized dance behind the bar.

When she was up, Samair ordered her drink and decided to do things the easy way. "Is Joey Kent here tonight?"

"Joey's here somewhere." Purple and black curls bobbed

as the bartender squeezed a lime into Samair's drink. "If you can't find her in the crowd, wait ten minutes and you'll see her in one of the cages. She never breaks for long."

That sounded like the Joey she knew. Full of fire and never far from a dance floor.

"Thanks." Samair put a ten dollar bill down and picked up her drink. "Keep the change."

"Anytime, sweetness," she replied with a wink and a grin completely at odds with her dark Goth look.

Glass in hand, Samair started the stroll around the club. A tingle of awareness danced up her spine and she looked over her shoulder but saw nothing unusual. She continued her walk around the club, heading for the dance floor, unable to shake the feeling that someone was watching her through the packed crowd.

Her blood hummed as it raced through her veins. Anger, determination, and excitement all combined to give her just the push she needed to take control of her life again.

For twenty-eight years she'd listened to her parents' lectures and had done her best to live up to their expectations. She took business courses in college instead of art or creative design, and she worked crappy hours in a small boutique just so she could be near what she really loved: clothes. She'd been undemanding in the bedroom, and put up with lousy sex so she could have a steady boyfriend.

Okay, so the putting up with crappy sex hadn't been part

of her parents' lectures, but having a steady relationship had been. And that meant putting up with mediocre sex.

Somehow after high school she'd done everything *proper*, and it had bitten her in the ass.

Well, she was done with it. It was time to do things her way, and she knew just the person to help her relearn what that was.

Just as Samair reached the far corner of the room she heard a piercing rebel yell and turned to see a striking redhead climb into one of the platform cages on the edge of the dance floor and start shaking her booty.

Despite the long, straight, brilliant red hair pulled back in two high pigtails, the neutral makeup, and the porcelain complexion, Joey Kent did not look innocent. Maybe it was the custom-made leather halter top, short shorts, and knee-high boots.

Whatever it was, it didn't matter. All that mattered was that Joey was there, and she was a friend.

Samair chuckled and made her way in that direction. She ran her hand up Joey's calf to her bare skin and tickled her behind the knee to get her attention. Joey swung around sharply, and saw Samair.

"Sammie!" The last vestiges of Samair's anger and frustration slipped away at the pure welcome in Joey's grin.

"Hey, baby!" Samair shouted.

"Get your butt up here, girl!"

Without thinking twice, Samair set her drink on the edge of the platform and tossed her worn leather backpack into the cage. She gripped the bars, hoisted herself up, and squeezed between the metal into the cramped space. And was instantly wrapped in her old friend's arms.

Joey must've picked up on something in her hug, because when she pulled back, there was concern in her expression. "What's wrong? What happened?"

Samair shook her head and flashed a wicked grin. "Later," she shouted. "For now I just want to have a good time!"

"Let's do it!"

Joey reached for the buttons of Samair's simple blouse and started to undo them while both girls moved to the music.

2

Samair closed her eyes, listened to the music, and let herself go. Joey's body rubbed against hers and the two girls danced as if they belonged together. As if it hadn't been almost three years since the last time.

Heat began to build inside her, and Samair opened her eyes to scan the mass of bodies on the dance floor. "It's a bit of a high, isn't it?" Joey's voice was husky as she moved closer.

Samair lost track of time as they danced with abandon, bumping and grinding against each other, lost in the flashing lights and loud music. The heat of many eyes landed on her, and she enjoyed every minute of it. Joey's soft and feminine hands floated over her generous curves, and Samair shifted closer as one of those hands slid under the cover of her hair. Joey put her forehead against Samair's, and the women gazed into each other's eyes.

"It's been a long time, Sammie." Joey's breath floated over her lips.

"It has," she replied, trailing her own hands teasingly over Joey's bare back as she writhed against her. "I'm sorry."

Both of Joey's hands cupped her head and she spoke clearly, "You never need to apologize to me. I'm just happy to see you."

Then she kissed her. A hard kiss on the lips that lingered for just a second. When they pulled apart, it was to hoots of approval and raucous clapping.

"Welcome back, Trouble."

They shifted apart, and Joey gave another piercing rebel yell. Samair's grin was a mile wide as she slipped between the bars of the cage and dropped back to the carpeted floor that edged the dance floor. Her heart was pounding and her breath came in pants, but she couldn't remember when she'd felt better.

Reaching between the bars, she grabbed her backpack from the floor of the cage and snagged the blouse she'd removed while dancing. After using it to pat her neck and upper chest dry, she reached for the drink she'd set aside earlier. The ice had melted but it quenched her thirst well enough.

A bead of sweat trickled between her breasts and she

thought about reaching down to wipe there, but reconsidered when she felt intent eyes still on her. She might not be shy, but she wasn't tacky either.

"You'd think they'd never seen a woman in a camisole before," she said when Joey dropped down to the floor beside her.

"It's not that. My God, look around you. Most of the time there's more bare skin in Risqué than on the beach." Joey laughed and threaded her arm around Samair's. "It's the fact that your camisole is this virginal white satin and lace thing that looks downright naughty at the same time. It's one of yours, isn't it?"

Samair nodded and felt a sting of pride. She'd made the top herself. Since the age of sixteen, her passion for sewing, combined with her curvy and slightly disproportionate body, had inspired her to create clothes for herself that fit *and* looked good—including lingerie.

"You don't think it might be because you stripped me of my blouse and then kissed me?"

"Ya think?" Joey giggled and steered her to a booth along the back wall where there was small group of people. "What can I say? I'm happy to see you."

While they walked Samair felt the hairs on the back of her neck rise and glanced around. Someone was watching her again. Closely.

"Everyone, this is Samair. Sammie, this is . . . everyone."

She laughed and waved a hand at the five others sitting in the booth.

"I'm Rob." The guy closest to her held out his hand. After shaking her hand, he pointed to each of the others as he rattled off their names. "That's Tara, Kelly, Jason, and Savannah."

Each was dressed to the nines, with a unique individual style that bared a lot of skin and cleavage. Samair figured they were some of Joey's dancer friends. The waitress arrived at the table and Joey ordered two tequilas and water. Samair added her order of two as well.

"One of those was for you," Joey said as they sat down.

"I know, but I want two, and you're going to keep up with me." She met her friend's raised eyebrows with a grin.

"Not a problem, little girl," Joey replied smartly. "So tell me what's new. I haven't talked to you in almost two months, and I haven't seen you in—Geez! In what—almost three years?"

"Something like that." Samair glanced around the table of strangers. Even though none of them appeared to be listening, she didn't want to talk about how her day had gone.

Hell, she didn't want to think about how her *life* had gone. She just wanted to be with someone who knew *her* and have a good time. "Can I tell you about it tomorrow?"

"Am I going to see you tomorrow?"

"Sure, I'm staying at your place for a while."

When Joey grinned and nodded, Samair relaxed and let out the breath she hadn't even been aware she was holding.

Joey had been the one who'd tried to keep them in contact. Samair had been too busy to go to the bar with her or even call her back half the time. It was her fault they'd lost contact, and she was thankful Joey wasn't the type of friend who would hold it against her.

"Excuse me." The waitress leaned over Samair's shoulder and she shifted in her seat so the girl could reach the table. She pulled some cash out of her pocket and the waitress shook her head. "The drinks are on the house."

Samair's eyebrows jumped in surprise. "Really?" she asked the pretty waitress. "Why?"

"Val said so, and what he says goes."

The waitress walked away before Samair could even tip her. She glanced at Joey. "Who's Val?"

"Valentine Ward." Joey raised her glass and nodded at the far corner. "He owns the club."

Samair's head swiveled and she searched the corner Joey had indicated, and collided with the super-intense gaze of the man there.

Even dressed in crisp pressed trousers and a tailored dress shirt, and with his strong masculine features softened by a small smile, he had a lean, lethal look about him. As if he were a barely tamed wild animal. Before she could get a really good look at him he stepped back, deeper into the shadows, but she could still feel the heat of his gaze on her.

A shiver danced down her spine.

"He doesn't mind you drinking while you work?"

He was the one who had been watching her; she knew it without a doubt.

"Not as long as we don't get smashed. You're fired if you get drunk, and he *always* knows when someone does."

Joey watched as Sammie laughed at one of Rob's ridiculous jokes. She'd never met the dancers Joey worked with before, but you'd never know it to see the way they all laughed and joked together.

It had always been like that. Sammie could walk into a room full of strangers and fifteen minutes later everyone was in love with her. There was just something about her that made people want to be with her.

Everyone wanted to be with Sammie, but only the guys wanted to be with Joey. For whatever reason, most women didn't like Joey. They especially didn't like Joey around their boyfriends, which was stupid because she'd never fool around with a guy who was taken.

Joey cringed inside. She didn't know what was wrong with her. Normally she was positive and enthusiastic about everything, but lately . . . It was probably just hormones. She'd been feeling a little lonely, so Sammie's timing was perfect.

It would be nice to have someone around to talk to.

Someone who saw beyond the flirtatious cage dancer persona that felt all too real lately.

A short time later, Samair came out of the ladies' room in time to see Valentine Ward climbing the stairs to the second floor. Unable to deny the impulse, she followed him.

It was getting late, close to the end of the night, and the stairs were empty. Almost everyone was either on the dance floor or cozying up to another warm body in a dark corner. She was on the bottom step just as he reached the top, and she got a quick view of fine cotton tightening over the perfect shape of his butt. How could a man's ass look that good in dress pants? Normally only tight denim or bare naked looked so yummy to her.

Sure, her blood had been running hot all night, but that sight made her breath catch and her fingers itch.

She climbed the stairs, her eyes tracking him as he crossed the floor. He waved at a blond guy with tattoos who sat at the bar in the small VIP section, but didn't slow his pace. He nodded at the bouncer watching over the sectioned-off space, then turn left and disappeared down a corridor she hadn't noticed earlier.

Throwing her shoulders back, she sauntered behind him, flashing the bouncer a small smile. When she entered the corridor, there was an open door at the end of it.

"Enjoying yourself tonight?" he asked when she entered the room.

He stood behind a large wooden desk, his head bent as he slid something into a drawer. She'd been silent, but he'd known she was there. Impressive.

"Yes, I am," Samair replied, stepping more fully into the office and looking around. "Are you?"

The room was very clean and modern, though not large. An overstuffed leather couch along one wall, some bookshelves, a closed door to the right of her and a floor-to-ceiling wall of windows on her left. It looked normal, yet the air in the room seemed to vibrate with an extraordinary energy. When the drawer of his desk snapped closed, she stopped fighting it and let her gaze focus on him.

Midnight-dark hair slicked back in a small ponytail only emphasized the strength of his features. Dark eyebrows over even darker eyes, and shadows of stubble along his jaw gave him an edgy, dangerous look. His stark handsomeness was completely masculine, except for the softness of full, sensuous lips that lifted at the corner before he spoke. "I'm about to enjoy it more."

He looked like a wolf in sheep's clothing, and the gleam in his eye told her she was the lamb he wanted.

3

Erotic heat surged through her and she realized that this was what she needed to forget the day from hell she'd had.

God, she wanted to wipe the past several years from her memory.

She'd all but lost herself in the tedious day-to-day existence of trying to be someone her parents would be proud of. Someone she wasn't. She knew forgetting it all was a tall order and would take both time and effort, but she was willing to start with just that day for now.

More than willing, she was *eager*.

"I wanted to thank you for the drinks you sent earlier. It was very nice of you." She moved around the room, running a finger along the books on the shelves but not seeing the titles.

"You're welcome." His deep voice sent a seductive shiver sizzling down her spine. He tilted his head, watching with a speculative stare as she prowled the room. "What is it you're looking for, Samair?"

That he knew her name should've surprised her. Yet it didn't. She doubted much got past this man, especially in his own club.

More times than she could count during her partying college years, Samair would walk by a hot guy in a club, smile at him flirtatiously, and have him grin back. Then he'd shake his head regretfully and say, "Oh man, you are trouble," before walking away.

There were different variations on the sentence, but for some reason, the refrence to *trouble* was always there. Valentine gave the impression of a man familiar with all sorts of trouble.

Just what she needed.

"Right now?" She shrugged. "Nothing. Today I figured out I wasn't doing what I really wanted to do, so I quit my job."

Why'd she tell him that? It's not like he'd care.

Sure enough, he skipped over her answer and went right to the heart of the matter. His full lips tilted up at one corner, and the temperature in the room inched higher. "What is it you *want* then?"

"Right now . . . I just want to have a good time."

"Is that all you want out of life? Fun?"

"No. But I don't want to think about the rest of my life right now."

Something like triumph flashed across his features, and adrenaline rushed through Samair's veins. She moved to the middle of the room, placed her hands on the empty surface of the desk between them, and leaned forward. "Why did you send over those drinks? Do you do that for all your customers?"

"Not all of them. As for why . . . I saw you walk in here tonight. You had the look of a woman on a mission." His wide shoulders lifted and fell as he spoke, his dark eyes never straying from her gaze. "I can't resist a woman who knows what she wants and goes after it."

"What if I told you that the mission I'm on is to do whatever I want to do, whenever I want to do it? And right now what I want is for you to fuck me. Would you still be unable to resist?"

The slight widening of his eyes was the only sign that she'd surprised him. Her sex heated and her juices began to flow. He was a man with self-control. The urge to see just what it would take to get a stronger reaction from him was secondary only to the hungry itch between her thighs.

He arched a lazy eyebrow. "That depends on why you want me."

Samair thought about this as he searched her face. She

straightened up and took a step back from the desk, willing to let him look his fill of her, confident in her sex appeal.

Everywhere he looked, her skin heated. It was if his hands were measuring the roundness of her hips, the heaviness of her breasts. They hadn't even touched, and she was almost ready to beg for his cock.

"They say the number one fantasy among women is sex with a stranger. You're a stranger." Unable to stop herself, she lifted a hand and trailed a fingertip across the top of her breast, dipping into her cleavage for a brief second before letting the hand fall to her side again. "I figure I'll start at the top of the list, and work my way down."

With a small nod that made her clit throb in anticipation, he turned sideways and pointed to a spot directly in front of him. "Come here."

The command in his voice made her head light. Enjoying the feel of her thighs rubbing together, the friction of the seam of her pants rubbing against her sensitive bits, she sauntered over to him. As eager as she was, part of her didn't want him to know how easily he affected her. When she reached the spot directly in front of him, she was trembling with excitement.

"Are you sure you want this?" His dark eyes were steady on hers. She wondered how he could possibly doubt she wanted this. Shit, she also wondered why she was taking orders instead of just jumping his bones. Yet she was.

She sucked her bottom lip between her teeth and bit down

on it, her fingers working the closure of her slacks, and pushing them and her panties over her hips with a quick wiggle.

"On the desk."

Hot skin met with the cool, polished desktop and a gasp escaped her. She sat straight, waiting for his next command, but he didn't speak again. Instead he stepped forward, spreading her thighs with his hip, and cradled her head in his hands. She fought to breathe as she watched him lower his head until their lips touched.

4

Every muscle in Val's body was hard as a rock when he got his first taste of the girl. The urge to bend her over the desk and fuck her so hard she couldn't walk was strong, but he didn't want to scare her away. He might be the stranger of her fantasy right now, but he already knew he wanted more than this one time with her.

A soft whimper sounded as her hands gripped his hips and her lips parted beneath his. She tasted so sweet, and just a bit tart. Her fingers dug into his hips harder and he opened his mouth, deepening the kiss.

Her tongue ducled with his, their panting breaths mingling as he tilted her head and changed angles. Needing more, he dragged his lips away and nibbled at her jaw, her neck, her earlobe. She tasted so good. He sucked in a deep breath and his control slipped an inch at the musky scent of sweat and aroused female. His heart pounded in his chest, and his cock threatened to burst through the seam of his pants.

He skimmed his hands over her curves. Cupping the weight of her breasts, he lifted them to his mouth, where he sucked at the hard tips through the thin satin of her camisole. As much as he liked the thin skimpy top more than the blouse she'd warn earlier, it was in his way now. He pulled the edge of it down, forcing it beneath her tits so they were plumped up and naked for his amusement. With a groan he gripped her spread thighs, pulled her to the edge of the desk, and clamped his lips around a rigid nipple.

Her cry of pleasure echoed through the room and he reached up and clamped a hand over her mouth. Her tongue flicked against the palm of his hand and her legs wrapped around his waist, aligning her hot wet core against his cotton-covered dick.

He bit down on a nipple experimentally and felt her stiffen and cry out against his hand. When he raised his head to make sure he hadn't hurt her, her big blue eyes were begging him. He removed his hand from her mouth just as her hand reached between their bodies and started in on his zipper.

"Fuck me. Now." She panted the words. "Please."

Val crushed her lips with his, swallowing her whimpers as he shoved her hands aside. He made quick work of his belt and pushed his pants out of the way. Pulling back a bit, he tore open the foil package he'd retrieved from his pocket and sheathed himself. Female claws dug into his naked hips, tugging at him while she writhed on his desk.

Christ, she was hot. She looked like a virgin eager to sin for the first time in nothing but her white satin and lace top. He squeezed the base of his dick and reached deep to find his center. It just took a second, and his control was solid again.

He stepped closer to rub the head of his cock between her swollen pussy lips. He grazed her clit and pushed lightly against her entrance. "Put your hands on the desk behind you."

When she hesitated, her fingers still gripping his hips and tugging him toward her, he pulled his cock away. "If you want this, do as I say."

Her eyes flew to his, her flush deepening as she placed her hands behind her, bracing herself. *Oh yeah, she likes to be told what to do.*

"Good girl," he murmured.

He placed his cock at her entrance and pushed forward gently. When she gasped and tried to rock forward, he shushed her. "You need to keep quiet. You didn't close the door when you came in here, and if you make too much noise, Marc will hear you over the music and come to see what's going on."

Her insides contracted around him and he stifled a groan

of his own. So, the thought of getting caught turned his little sinner on.

The music from the club could barely be heard in the office since he'd turned his speakers off when he entered, but he knew it would be loud out on the landing. He also knew there was no way his bouncer would hear them from the VIP door thirty feet away and around a corner. And even if Marc did, he wouldn't leave his post. But instinct had made him taunt her, and it paid off.

Gripping her hips tightly, he held her in place while he slowly eased inside her. Inch by inch, he filled her up, feeling her tight cunt stretch around him until he was in deep, her insides twitching around him. Reaching with both hands he cupped the pretty breasts that were thrust forward by her position, the flushed nipples hard and begging for attention.

He eased out, and back in, keeping his pace slow and steady. He watched as her head fell back, her hair almost touching the desk as she clamped her lips tight and whimpered.

"What is it, baby? What do you want?"

He watched her eyes flutter open. She lifted her head, pleading with him silently. Her lips parted and for an instant he wanted to be fucking her mouth instead. She bit her bottom lip and another whimper filled the room. "Come on baby, tell me what you want."

"Harder," she gasped out.

Val bit back a grin and thrust deep, his hips slapping

against her inner thighs. She cooed her delight and he slid a hand past her breast to her shoulder.

"You like that? You like it hard?" His hips picked up speed, slamming into her. "You like it a little rough?"

She moaned and her cunt sucked at him, giving him an answer. His balls drew up tight and he pumped faster, harder. God, it felt good! His fingers squeezed a nipple, hard, and his other hand slid from her shoulder to her neck. His hand tightened slowly around her throat, and he watched her face carefully as he kept up a fast and hard rhythm with his hips.

Her eyes popped open and one hand left the desk to grip his wrist when she realized her air supply was slowly getting cut off. A touch of panic flared in the depths of her blue eyes a split second before they shut again and her cunt clamped down hard on his cock and her wetness flooded him.

He relaxed his light grip on her throat, and grabbed her hips. With one last thrust he went as deep as he could, and let go.

oly shit! Samair fell back on the desk, a hand over her heart. *What the hell just happened?*

Valentine pulled away slowly and she heard the rustle of clothes and his belt buckle jingle. Taking a deep breath, she sat up and slid off the desk, not looking at him. She braced one hand on the desk, and bent down to pick up her slacks. The same pants she'd worn to her hated job that morning.

So much had happened since then.

She stepped carefully into her pants, pulling them over her shoes, before straightening and zipping them up. She bent down again, grabbed her panties, and stuffed them into her pocket. She was about to step around the desk when a large hand grasped her elbow and pulled her against a warm hard body.

"You okay?" His deep voice rumbled against her ear.

Samair nodded and wrapped her arms around his waist.

After a minute of silent snuggling, he pulled her away from him gently. A warm finger lifted her chin until she was looking him in the eye.

"You're amazing." He pressed a quick kiss to her lips then turned away.

Samair took a last peek at his perfect ass then spun on her heel and sashayed out of the room. Confident, once again in control, and satisfied.

Trouble was back.

5

Val turned his head and watched Samair's curvy hips swing as she left his office. Last call was over and the lights were up in the bar. She'd been with the dancers earlier, and they usually sat at their table until the bouncers ushered them out. He saw her saunter down the stairs and across the floor to rejoin them, and wondered what it would be like to have her dance for him.

Privately.

"You work fast."

Val glanced away from the wall of windows and gave the man entering his office a small smile.

Growing up in the foster care system had taught Val not to trust easily. But fifteen years earlier Karl had come upon

Val in a street fight against some guys who hadn't liked the outcome of their pool tournament. Karl hadn't liked the four-to-one odds, and jumped in, saving Val's ass. They'd both cleaned up some since then, but they'd had each others backs ever since.

Val trusted him, and that was saying something.

"I didn't work at all; she came to me." He couldn't stop the grin that spread across his face.

"Damn man, what is it that makes women throw themselves at you?"

"What makes them throw themselves at *you*?" he shot back.

"My good looks and roguish charm." Karl laughed. They both knew women loved the way he looked. And they both knew that he was rarely charming.

"For this woman, it was the chance to live a fantasy."

They both watched as Samair and the redheaded dancer, Joey, left together almost immediately after Samair rejoined the group.

"God bless women who want to live out their fantasies," Karl said softly.

Val clapped him on the shoulder before turning back to his desk, but didn't say anything. He sat down and looked at the other man.

A few months earlier, Karl had met a special woman who'd also been bent on living out a fantasy or two. Things with Katie hadn't turned out the way Karl had hoped, and even though he never said much about it, Val knew his friend had been disappointed.

"You gonna to see her again?" Karl asked.

"Probably." *Definitely.* He tilted his chair back and studied the guy in front of him. "What?"

"I don't think it's a good idea, man." Karl shook his head slowly. "You're too close to hitting the mark and owning the club free and clear. Getting distracted right now is not the thing to do."

"She's not a distraction. She's entertainment."

"Uh-huh."

Determination filled him. "Trust me on this, Karl. Nothing will distract me from keeping this club out of Vera's reach. It's always been mine, and it will always *be* mine."

"It's not yours until you make the final payment and the bank loan is paid. Damn it, Val! I told you it was stupid to not go after her for more in the divorce. She cheated on you, and you let her get away with it."

"I didn't let her get away with it. I left her." Why didn't Karl understand that when it came to Vera, her cheating had hurt him way more than her money could ever heal him?

He'd grown up fast and hard, and he'd mistaken Vera's honeyed words and warm body for a warm heart and, finally, a home.

During the year they were married Val never accepted a

dime from his rich wife, and when he walked out the door of their house for the last time, he'd taken nothing with him but the clothes on his back, his precious Harley, and the keys to the club. "I only wanted what I'd gone into the marriage with. The rest wasn't worth anything to me."

"I'll never understand how you got suckered by her." Karl shook his head and dropped into the chair in front of the desk.

It was simple really. He'd wanted her, he'd loved her, then he'd trusted her.

He'd been stupid.

"If you don't clear the mortgage by the deadline, the bank will foreclose."

"I know that," Val snapped before scrubbing a hand down his face. He swallowed a sigh and spoke again. "Sorry, man. Just talking about it makes my skin crawl."

"I know, buddy. I wish I could help you out more, but—"

"You've done all you can." Val waved his hand sharply, cutting Karl off. "And I promise you, your investment is safe."

"I don't give a damn about the money."

"Just the same, it's safe. I've given Vera enough. She can use all the influence her family has, but I *will not* forfeit this club."

6

Samair woke slowly, the knowledge that she wasn't alone in the bed creeping into her consciousness. She rolled away from the warm body she'd been cuddled against and landed on the floor. On her ass. Hard.

"Ouch!" She pushed a lock of hair out of her eyes and glared at the figure still sound asleep in the bed. Some things never changed; Joey always had been a heavy sleeper. And a bed hog.

Samair stumbled to her feet and headed for the bathroom. After a long warm shower, with a quick blast of cold at the end, she felt awake. Almost.

She stood in the middle of the small studio apartment, pulling on her dress pants from the night before—sans underwear once again—when Joey's eyes popped open and she jumped out of bed, instantly awake.

"I hate you," Samair muttered.

"I love you, too."

Joey grinned as she made quick work of making the bed. "Still not a morning person, eh?"

"It's dark out. Mornings are not supposed to be dark."

Since the club hadn't stopped playing music until after two in the morning and Joey wouldn't leave while she could still dance, they'd gotten home only a few hours ago. The good thing about that was they'd fallen straight into bed with nothing more than muttered goodnights.

Joey laughed softly as she made her way to the bathroom. "It's almost October, what do you expect?"

"It's not winter yet!"

"Will be soon," Joey singsonged over the sound of the shower. Samair knew she was right, too. The days were getting shorter, and the nights longer. At least in Vancouver they didn't get tons of snow all winter long like the rest of Canada.

As Samair passed the open bathroom door, Joey stuck her head out from the shower. "Put the kettle on, would you? And be prepared to spill your guts when I get out."

Samair had known Joey would only give her so much time before she'd start demanding to know why her friend had suddenly reappeared.

The cab ride home the night before had been full of hushed giggles and light flirting as only friends who had once been lovers could achieve. There'd been no inquisition, only open acceptance. They'd been best friends for the four years of college, but had drifted apart over the years since. Yet Joey's open welcome the night before made it crystal clear to Samair that their friendship wasn't affected by things like distance.

So, she'd tell her friend everything.

She went into the kitchen, filled the shiny kettle with water, and set it on the stove. Then she filled the glass she'd pulled from the cupboard with Diet Coke and leaned against the countertop. She stared unseeingly at the small studio apartment, the events of the night before coming back to her in a rush.

She leaned against the wall just inside her apartment, her fingers gripping the leather backpack she always carried with her, and gaped at the scene playing out before her.

Kevin's begging echoed through the room and cut through the roaring in her head. "Yes, Mistress . . . More please . . . Yes . . . I'm yours."

Samair stared for a full minute. Her clean-cut boyfriend was naked and bent over the back of the living room couch as her roommate, Lisa, flexed her hips and shafted him with a big black strap-on.

*She finally summoned enough breath to speak.
"Well, this explains a lot," she said loud enough to be
heard over the sound of bodies slapping together.*

*Kevin's head jerked up in surprise and he tried to
straighten from his position bent over the back of the
sofa. The fact that his hands were cuffed behind his
back, and that Lisa kept him pinned there with her
hips, made his efforts futile.*

"Samair! You're home early!"

*"I quit my job." Well, wasn't that a good come-
back.*

*She stiffened her knees and straightened up, mov-
ing away from the wall. Ignoring the malicious glint
in Lisa's eyes, she spoke as casually as she could
manage.*

*"You knew the whole time why our sex life
sucked, didn't you?"*

*Lisa rested a possessive hand on Kevin's lower
back and shrugged her delicate shoulders. "I knew
what Kevin really wanted, and I knew you'd never give
it to him. I didn't see any reason why I shouldn't."*

*"Well . . . now you can 'give it to him' all the time.
I'm done with you both."*

Samair gave her head a shake. It was over and done with.
In the space of a few hours, she'd managed to toss away ev-

erything she'd worked for over the past few years. Shit, she didn't even have clean clothes to wear!

Or a place to live.

She could probably stay with Joey for a while, but it was a really tiny apartment. Basically one room, with only a breakfast bar separating the kitchen from the main area, and a curtain separating the bedroom. The curtain was open right now and from where she stood leaning on the bar Samair could see the bed and clothes on the floor. At least the bathroom had a door on it.

Not that it mattered, since Joey hadn't closed it and Samair could clearly hear her off-key singing.

One thing she knew for sure, she wasn't going back. She'd pick up some of her stuff from her old apartment, enough to get by, but that was it. Even though the apartment was in her name, she'd let Lisa have it *and* Kevin.

Her mind was made up: It was time for a life change. She'd be okay staying with Joey for a short time while she figured out what the next step was, but the place was way too small for a visit much longer than that.

Yet since it was so small, the rent should be reasonable. She could probably get herself a place just like it. It would have everything she needed. Of course, she needed to find a new job first.

She banged her forehead lightly against the kitchen countertop. *Fucked, fucked, I'm fucked.*

"Stop that before you hurt yourself." Joey strode from the bathroom to the bed area, naked. "Are you gonna tell me what's going on?"

Samair ignored her question and asked one of her own as she watched her friend pull a pair of yoga pants on over a pair of nylon short shorts. A heavy sweatshirt then covered her sparkly Lycra sports bra. "You still teaching?"

"Five classes a day, five days a week. I'm a professional now." She grinned. "But I'm not teaching today. I heard about an open call for dancers for a video shoot, so I'm going to audition."

"Shit, you dance at the club. You've been a professional for years. You'll ace the audition."

"It's a bar. It's not the same thing."

"You had to audition to be a dancer there though, right?"

"Yes"

"Then it's a job. You're a professional. Not everyone can do that, stop selling yourself short."

"And *you* stop avoiding me," Joey said as she moved around the counter and poured the hot water for her tea. "You're going to spill your guts to me right now. I don't have time to fuck around."

Samair sighed. "To sum everything up, I've finally decided to stop pretending to be someone I'm not. To stop pretending I'm happy with a mediocre job and a mediocre boyfriend."

"And what brought on this epiphany?"

The fact that Joey didn't ask what she'd meant didn't escape Samair's notice.

"My boss pissed me off and I walked out on my job only to get home early enough to find Kevin getting fucked up the ass with a strap-on by my so-called friend."

Joey's jaw dropped, then she started to howl with laughter. "Oh my god! You're kidding!"

"Nope."

Joey laughed until tears leaked from her eyes. Taking deep breaths, she eyed Samair closely. When she could talk without giggling she spoke. "Are you okay? I mean, how much did you love this guy?"

Samair smiled, seeing the humor in it all now that the shock had worn off. "I'm fine. I mean . . . I was shocked, angry even . . . but strangely, not hurt. After I told them what I thought of them I walked around for a bit, and I realized that I actually didn't really care about any of the stuff that had happened. I'd pretty much reacted to it the way I *thought* I should, but really, I didn't care." She shook her head slowly. "I haven't cared about anything for a while now."

"Oh sweetie," Joey reached out and grabbed her hand, linking their fingers together. As if she could read Samair's mind, she scolded her gently. "Just because you're not heartbroken over those idiots doesn't mean you don't care. It just means that they didn't surprise you. That, deep down, you never expected anything more from them than what you got. Unfortunately, with your family, you've learned to expect less than true honesty from people."

"I expect true honesty from you."

"That's because you and I are soul sisters, babe." Joey winked at her over her mug of tea. "You know me as well as I know you."

Joey was right. They'd seen each other for the first time in close to three years last night, and it had felt like no time at all. It didn't matter that she'd basically ditched Joey to focus on building a life she really hadn't wanted; they knew each others' hearts and secrets. They *were* soul sisters.

"What did your boss do to piss you off? You've been working there since I met you. I thought you loved Bethany."

"I do love Beth. Unfortunately for me, she got pregnant last year and left. Rosa, the owner has been running the shop while Beth is on maternity leave, and she's a stuck-up bitch who doesn't know anything about fashion."

Joey laughed. "Tell me how you really feel."

"She just reminded me too much of my mom. Nothing I did was ever good enough. She pushed a button and I went off." Samair smiled. "It sure felt good to tell her to fuck off though."

"For the sake of your sanity, you gotta do that every now and then." She shrugged. "So what's the plan now?"

"I've no idea. Can I stay with you for a while?"

The look Joey gave her made it clear she was an idiot for even asking. She set down her tea and wrapped Samair in a quick hug before slipping into her shoes and grabbing her gym bag.

"There's a computer in that corner cabinet and an extra set of apartment keys in the mug with the pens and pencils. Take them. I'll be back around three. See you then!" And she was gone.

7

A car horn honked and Samair stopped short with one foot still on the curb.

Shit, she'd better pay more attention or she was going to get run over. Between the dreary rain and the three hours of going through the job databank at the employment office, she was in a bit of a mental fog. Glancing around, she saw a Starbucks across the street and headed straight for it.

She carried a steaming mug of coffee to a small table near the window and had just sat down when her cell phone rang.

When she saw the caller ID she was tempted to ignore it. Instead, she swallowed a sigh and flipped open the phone. "Hi, Cherish, what's up?"

"Samair, are you okay?" Her sister's words were rushed, her voice worried. Cherish was only two years older than Samair, but she'd always acted like a second mother.

"Of course I'm okay. Why wouldn't I be?"

"I called Rosa's and she said she'd fired you. What happened?"

"I didn't get fired. I quit." Samair glanced around the coffee shop; a few people were talking on phones, and with the rain outside the place was so busy her conversation wouldn't bother anyone. She might as well get it over with; she was going to have to deal with her family sooner or later. "And you may as well know I broke up with Kevin, and I'm moving out of the apartment, too, so tell Mom and Brett if they want to get a hold of me, they should call my cell."

"You're moving, too? What's going on? Where are you going to live? Are you having a nervous breakdown?"

"No. I'm fine, everything is fine." She swirled the stir stick in her coffee. "It's just time for a change."

"A change?"

A heavy sigh echoed in Samair's ear and she closed her eyes. Here it comes.

"What could you possibly want to change? You have a great job, a boyfriend, and a nice apartment in a very nice neighborhood. You have everything you could want, Samair."

"No, I had everything *you* could want. Everything Mom wanted us to have. But it wasn't what *I* wanted."

There was a moment of silence after Samair's words. That Samair had been different from her siblings wasn't a secret. Cherish was the smart, perfect one. Their younger brother Brett was the athletic, charming one. And Samair, the middle child, was the chubby, flaky one.

Cherish pushed forward. "Todd can probably get you a job in his office as an—"

"I don't want to work for your husband."

More silence. She could almost see Cherish sitting at her perfect kitchen table in her perfect house, shaking her head in bewilderment.

"I'm doing what I want to do, Cherish. I'm twenty-eight years old. Don't you think it's about time?"

"Where are you moving to? What are you going to do about a job? Samair—have you thought any of this through?"

Samair knew from experience the conversation was only going to go downhill from there. "I'm staying with Joey, and I'll find a job. There are plenty of clothing stores out there." So what if most were chain stores that wouldn't allow her any freedom to alter the clothes for the clients?

To be honest, she was sick and tired of letting other people tell her what she could and couldn't do. The ultimate plan would be to open her own store, but she couldn't even afford to rent an apartment, let alone start a business.

As she looked out the window, Samair listened with half an ear to her sister babble on about what Mom would think, and question why she would want to work in a clothing store when she had a college education. "You might be a bit flaky but you're such a smart girl, Samair. You could do so much better than working as a salesgirl in some retail outlet."

Tired of banging her head against a brick wall, Samair brought the conversation to a close. "I have to go now, Cherish. Tell Mom I'll call her in a couple of days. And don't worry, I'm fine."

Samair stared at the people around her. Everyone doing their own thing, minding their own business. No one had heard Cherish's harangue, but it was embarrassing just the same. It had been years since she'd been lectured like that. There'd been no lectures because she'd been a complete wuss. She'd stayed at a job when her new boss walked all over her, and she'd ignored the lack of chemistry with her boyfriend just because she thought she *should* be in a relationship.

Why she'd done that, she didn't know.

Yes, actually, she did know. She'd never really wanted a relationship, but after college, when she'd gotten a solid job—it *had been* a good, solid job when Bethany was running the boutique—a boyfriend seemed like the next step.

She'd been following the same plan the rest of her upper-middle-class family followed. And she'd gotten herself stuck in a relationship that was false and, by a twist of fate, a job where she was unappreciated.

Basically, she'd gotten a life she didn't really want.

She glared at the cold mug of coffee in front of her. She'd ordered it because it was what one did at a coffee shop, but she hated coffee. She hated the smell of it, the taste of it . . . she hated it.

Damn it!

She stood up so abruptly her chair fell back onto the floor and people stared. But she didn't care. She was done caring what others thought of her behavior. Last night, for the first time in way too long, she'd felt good.

She used to enjoy life. She used to be someone who had friends, plans . . . dreams. She used to feel things. Sometime in the past few years she'd lost her way. She'd given up on those things. She'd given up on herself, and settled.

Sure, she'd been a little impetuous, even a little wild, but she'd been alive. She'd been in charge of what she did and what happened to her. No one else, just her.

Just like she'd been last night.

She'd felt playful and daring when she'd hit the club, and even better when she'd gotten Valentine Ward alone.

Holy hell, that had been better than good!

A laugh bubbled up inside and spilled from her lips as she grabbed her backpack and headed for the door. She'd been her own boss, and she'd liked it. There was absolutely no reason why she couldn't go after her dream of *always* being her own boss.

8

Joey didn't bother with her keys when she got to her building. Instead she pushed the buzzer for her apartment and yelled, "It's me. Let me in."

The door buzzed and she pulled it open and started to climb the three flights of stairs. The audition had been long and grueling. She'd made it through the first three cuts, but not the final one. It totally sucked because she'd made it that far in auditions before, too many times to count, but she'd yet to get the break she needed.

Sometimes she wanted to give up. Sometimes she wondered if her love of dancing was enough, if maybe she just wasn't good enough to make it. In two more years she'd be thirty. Too old to be the kind of dancer she wanted to be. She enjoyed teaching—up to a point. But her heart was really in performing.

As much fun as dancing at Risqué was, she wanted more than that. She wanted to go on tour with a troupe or a show. Or at the least do some music videos or commercials. Vancouver's film industry was booming and there were plenty of opportunities; all she needed was the right break.

She was glad not to be alone with her thoughts that night. It was sort of nice to know someone was there waiting for her. Especially nice that it was Sammie.

She hadn't seen Samair in way too long. In all honesty, she'd wondered if she might never see her again.

The last time they'd hung out, Sammie had seemed so distant, and . . . well, sort of limp. Like all the life had gone out of her. But last night it was back full force, and Sammie had been as seductive as ever.

It sucked that the shit had hit the fan in Sammie's life, but it was good to see her friend's fire hadn't disappeared.

Just thinking about it made Joey feel a bit better. There was a time when she'd been in love with Samair. But that had changed. Romantic love had shifted sometime during their college explorations, morphing into a deep, abiding friendship. And Joey was going to do everything she could to help her friend follow her heart.

After all, she thought as she pushed open her apartment

door and hefted the plastic bags she was carrying onto the counter, life was meant to be *lived*.

One look around the studio apartment showed her that Sammie had indeed moved in. A couple of suitcases were lying on the bed, and Sammie was glued to the loveseat in front of her sewing machine, which was set up on the coffee table.

"Been busy today, have you?" She tossed her gym bag onto the bed next to Samair's suitcases. "I brought Chinese."

"Yum!" Samair said, cutting some threads and pulling her newest creation from the machine. After she ran a critical eye over it she tossed the material at Jocy. "Try this on."

"Ohhh! For me?" Pleasure ran through her and she squealed like a little girl. She *loved* it when Sammie made her clothes. They always fit perfectly, looked good, and lasted forever.

"Made just for you, baby."

All her depressing thoughts floated away while she whipped her sweatshirt over her head and did up the bra-like top as she walked toward the bathroom.

She pulled the door closed and gazed at herself in the full-length mirror hanging there.

"It's gorgeous, Sammie!" She ran her hands over the royal purple satin that cupped her breasts lovingly before she tangled her fingers in the soft fringe that hung from under the underwires to her hips. "You are so talented. When are you going to realize people would pay a lot to have something like this?"

She did a shimmy and a little bump and grind, loving the way the fringe played peekaboo with her fair skin. The top was going to help her rake in the tips.

"You really believe that?"

"Fuck yeah!"

"Good." Sammie's voice was determined. "Because I want you to help me start my own design label."

That got her attention. She spun away from the reflection in the mirror. "Really?"

Samair nodded.

"It's about time!" Joey left the mirror and grabbed Samair in an enthusiastic hug. She felt like a proud mama. Sammie was finally going to go after her dream and do what she was meant to do—be her own creative and original self.

This was exactly what Sammie needed. To remember what her dream was, and to go after it. When a person gives up on their dreams, their spirit dies.

She went back and looked in the mirror again. This time Joey looked herself in the eye. It didn't matter how many auditions she had to go to, she wasn't going to give up on her dream either.

Her stomach rumbled and she spun around and pointed at the waiting food. "You get that out while I change. Then we can eat, and you can tell me how I can help."

They didn't bother with plates, just used forks to eat straight out of the takeout containers as they brainstormed.

"I'll be your official model and spokesperson! I have a few things you've made me over the years, and I'll be sure to wear them, and tell everyone how durable they are, too. Durability is a key issue for dancers." Sweat and constant rubbing against body parts were hell on materials.

"I think starting with the dance community is great, but I need to do more. That isn't enough business." Samair chewed a piece of ginger chicken before rambling on. "I need to find a way to get the word out about custom lingerie, too. I know I'm not the only woman with hips and a big ass out there who wants to wear sexy underwear and not feel like an idiot."

"What about a catalogue?" She could leave one at the studio where she taught, and drop them off at every audition she went to. Soon they'd be all over the city.

But Sammie was quick to nix that idea.

"Too expensive. I have enough savings so that, if you agree to let me stay here, I won't have to look for a day job for a couple of months. But only if I'm smart about where I spend."

"*Mi casa es su casa.*" Joey waved her fork blithely. The place wasn't big, but she didn't need a lot of room and it was nice to have Sammie around again.

Samair grinned her thanks. "You know that means you get your outfits for free."

"Yes!"

"I want to make some low-slung black velvet hip-hugger

pants to go with the purple bra, too. Will you wear them to the club when you dance and tell all your friends to order some?"

"Ohh, velvet pants," she cooed. "Very cool. And for sure I'll push them for you. Okay, a catalogue is out, but you definitely need business cards! I can do some up for you on the computer as soon as we come up with a label."

Samair nibbled on her bottom lip. "What do you think of Trouble?"

"It's perfect." Joey set down her fork and raised her glass of Diet Coke in salute. "To doing what we were meant to do . . . and mucho success for Trouble!"

9

Val stood in the shadowed corner watching Samair as she danced. Things had been pretty hectic the last few days with staff problems, calls from Vera, and a visit to the courthouse to testify about a fight that had happened outside the club six months earlier. All normal things, but everything seemed to be happening at once, and the curvaceous blonde had popped into his head at odd times. He'd be doing the schedules or talking on the phone with his liquor vendor and the image of her on his desk, all angelic and naughty at the same time, would fill his mind.

He hadn't lied when he told Karl he wasn't going to let her distract him, but since she'd walked into Risqué that night he'd been able to think of nothing other than learning more of her secret fantasies.

The club was pretty busy for a Monday night, and he'd watched from his office as she laughed and danced with her friends until the itch under his skin became undeniable. After a quick round of the club, checking in with his doormen and bartenders to see that all was well, he'd found a corner and searched her out with his gaze.

A soft pink top hugged her upper body and showed off her fantastic cleavage, and a long flowing skirt hid the curve of her delectable ass. Her breasts bounced and her skirt swung as she danced with an enthusiasm and abandon that called to the animal deep within him.

As if she sensed his thoughts, she spun around and her gaze landed directly on the corner where he stood. On him.

There was no way she could see him in the darkened corner, but she knew someone was there, watching her. A defiant and blatantly devilish grin spread across her face and she shook her ass, rubbing against her partner. The challenge in her gaze was clear. She was out to have a good time, and nothing was going to get in her way.

She raised her hands, spun in her partner's arms, did a last rub against him, then walked away, leaving behind the loser who'd been trying to make a move on her on the dance floor.

The thrill of the chase fired up inside Val and he stepped out of the shadows to follow her. If she really wanted to misbehave, he was the man for her.

He saw her at the back bar and moved in that direction. When he stepped up behind her, Tommy was just sliding her drink in front of her. With a shake of his head Val signaled the bartender to refuse her money. Before she could turn around, he leaned in and spoke softly against her ear. "What's number two?"

She did a tight turn, her body brushing erotically against his, and looked up at him. "Number two?"

"On your list of favorite sexual fantasies."

"Oh, *that*." Her baby blue eyes met his dead on. "You thinking of helping me experience the whole thing?"

"Possibly."

Her little pink tongue snuck out and slid slowly over her pouty bottom lip, making his cock twitch with need.

Samair saw the flare of heat in Valentine's dark eyes and an answering flame licked at her insides. The urge to dance close to the fire had her reaching out to place a hand low on his belly. His stomach contracted, and heat seeped through the silk of his dress shirt to her fingertips, invading her body.

"I'm not so sure 'possibly' is good enough. You're asking me to share my deepest desires. They're very personal." She struggled to keep her voice light and flirtatious.

"How about we make a little deal?"

"Deal?"

He moved closer, leaving mere millimeters of space between their bodies as he reached up to brush a lock of hair away from her cheek. "You tell me your fantasies . . . and I'll make them come true."

Samair swallowed. Her heart pounded and her insides melted at his touch. She'd known from the first time she set eyes on him that he was a powerful man. Her time in his office, in his arms, had made her hyper-aware of just what kind of passion she'd been missing out on. This was no boy to be toyed with. If she said yes, there was no backing out. Mind you, he was offering her sex, not love, and not a relationship. He was offering her the perfect affair.

Valentine Ward was all man. Just being near him set her body to humming with erotic anticipation. His words promised untold pleasures and his steady gaze made it clear he was confident in his abilities to follow through.

Yet she couldn't help but try to push a button or two of her own. She smiled slowly and lifted a hand to play with the button at his neck. "Promises, promises."

He stepped back and tucked his hands into his pockets. His hooded gaze ran over her, making all her pleasure points tingle, and threw out a challenge of his own. "Are you brave enough to see if I can keep my promises?"

Nope, definitely not a boy.

A thrill ripped through her at the prospect of having this *man* do whatever she wanted. "Right now my fantasy is to have you on your knees, with your face buried between my thighs."

"Done."

10

Excitement swamped Samair as Val took her by the elbow and confidently led her through the crowd. Heart racing, nipples hardening, body softening in all the right places, she was ready to play.

They passed by the dance floor and Samair glanced over the crowd. Joey was watching her from the cage not ten feet away. Samair flashed her the thumbs-up and went back to concentrating on putting one foot in front of the other.

As far as sexual fantasies went, oral sex wasn't very daring. But it was the first thing to pop into her head and out of her mouth. Thinking straight when Val was standing right in front of her, offering to make her every fantasy come true, was a hard thing to do.

He was basically a stranger, and for sure was only interested in sex, but she couldn't seem to say no. And why should she? She'd already made the decision to start living life, and going after what *she* wanted. He'd seen her naked and panting before, he knew she was a little overweight, and he still wanted more. This time she hadn't gone to him—he'd come to her.

She'd have to be a freaking imbecile to say no!

Instead of going up the stairs to his office like she'd expected, he directed her underneath them to a dark door that blended with the wall.

Without a word he pulled a set of keys from his pocket, unlocked the door, and ushered her in. The room was dimly lit, and Samair was shocked to see how large it was

Plump sofas and low chairs were scattered about the floor space, and a small bar in the far corner told her the room was used for private parties.

A window that was about three feet high ran the length of one wall, and when Samair stepped closer she realized that the window was actually the mirror that ran the length of the dance floor.

"Wow," she whispered. "I never even knew this was here."

"It's mostly used for bachelor parties and such, but right now, it's perfect for what I have in mind." He stepped behind her, one strong arm circling her waist, his other hand tangling in her hair and pulling her head back for his kiss.

His body pressed against her backside while his lips covered hers. All thought fled from her brain as her lips parted naturally and she drank in the taste of Val.

She tried to turn in his arms, but he held her tight to him. His hardening cock pressed against her butt and she arched into it, wiggling and pressing back. Wanting to forget about the oral sex fantasy and just be taken by him. Filled by him.

"Hands on the window," he said, scraping his teeth lightly across her cheek and to her ear. He nipped at the fleshy lobe and goose bumps rose on her skin. "And don't move them."

His arm slid from around her waist and his chest scraped along her backside as he sank to his knees behind her. A gasp escaped when his firm hands clasped her ankles and urged her feet back and out. Before she knew it she was bent forward at the waist, her hands on the window keeping her standing as his hands slid up her outer thighs, lifting her skirt.

"Very nice," he said when her pink velvet thong was exposed. His words caused his hot breath to whisp over her buttocks, and a tremor of pure *want* ran through her as he quickly got rid of the panties.

Samair lifted her head and focused on the tableau of dancers on the other side of the one way mirror. She was afraid if she didn't that her knees would give out too soon, and she wouldn't get what she'd really been craving: Val's mouth on her body.

His hands ran up and down her legs, and then over her

rounded butt, lifting and squeezing her cheeks. Hot air landed on her exposed pussy lips a split second before a firm wet tongue speared between them. A joyous cry leapt from her throat and her knees trembled.

Val's grip on her hips was strong, his head thrust between her thighs as he showed no mercy. This was no gentle seduction. His mouth was firm, open and hungry. His thumbs spread her wide, his tongue thrust deep, and his teeth nipped teasingly. A thrilling mix of pain and pleasure whipped through her and her head fell forward, eyes closed. Who was she kidding? Nothing could distract her from what he was doing.

She was no innocent; men had eaten her out before. But she'd always felt too self-conscious to lie there, stretched out in such a vulnerable position, and stopped them after just a few minutes. Maybe it was standing up that made this so much better. Maybe it was facing the wall. Maybe it was Val and his blatant enjoyment of what he was doing. She didn't really care.

All she cared about was what she was feeling.

A finger circled her clit and his tongue toyed with her entrance, dipping in and out. Arousal coiled low in her belly and she arched her back, giving him better access. The pressure on her clit intensified and she ground down on him, her whole body straining toward the orgasm that was so close. Her fingers curled against the glass, trying to grab hold of something solid as the sensations built to an unbearable level and pleasure exploded through her. With a victorious cry she welcomed wave after wave of sensation as it flooded her mind and body.

Her knees buckled, but Val held her up, not stopping his attentions or giving her a chance to recover. Just when she was getting ready to beg him to stop, he shifted. His hand left her clit, a finger thrust deep inside her, and his tongue brushed lightly over her puckered rear hole. Her body jerked in response and he chuckled.

"So sensitive. I love that in a woman," he murmured.

"Never . . . Nobody's . . . ever . . . done that to me before." She forced the words out before a moan of pleasure ripped through her. She was hypersensitive.

"Hmmm," he hummed, sending small vibrations through her.

"Val . . ."

Another hum from him, another shudder ripping through her.

"Val . . . please."

She wasn't even aware of the words leaving her mouth. All she knew was that she wanted—she *needed* . . . more.

She continued to mutter, to beg and arch her back. She spread her legs farther as his hand rubbed faster, two fingers sinking deeper inside her as his tongue swirled around her back entrance until she snapped. "Val! Fuck me, damn it!"

"All you had to do was ask, baby."

Cool air flowed over her heated skin when he stood back. She heard nothing but the pounding of hot blood rushing through her veins until his hands once again gripped her hips and the head of his cock slid along her cleft.

"Yes!"

He thrust true, filling her up. With no hesitation he pumped fast and hard. His belly slapped against her ass and her breasts bounced as she braced herself against the window, reveling in his complete possession of her. Her insides spasmed and he groaned . . . so she deliberately tightened her inner muscles and thrust back against him again.

"God, you're hot!" he muttered.

One hand left her hip to slide over her belly and cup a swinging breast. He tugged at the edge of her stretchy velvet tank until she spilled over the neckline of the top and filled his hand. After a quick squeeze he focused on the nipple and pumped his hips harder . . . faster . . . harder. He slid his other hand low over her belly until his fingers landed on her clit and she went off in his arms.

Every muscle in her body tensed and a scream ripped from her throat, his guttural grunt of release mixing with hers.

Val fought to get his breath back, the sporadic spasming of Samair's cunt still massaging his softening cock and making his knees weak. *Christ, that felt good!*

His head fell forward to rest between her shoulder blades. The fact that she was still trembling in his arms and panting herself made him feel ten feet tall. This young, adventurous, wild thing was just what he needed after a marriage to a cold-hearted bitch who had gotten off on using his dick to control him.

In this new arrangement with Samair Jones, he was definitely the more experienced of the two, and he liked it that way.

"Val?"

The softly spoken query caused him to straighten up sharply. "Right here, babe." He stifled a groan as he pulled away from her soft warmth.

When she didn't speak again he cupped her shoulders and pulled her up and back against his chest. She really was something. He placed a soft kiss on her cheek, heard her sigh as she snuggled back against him and they both looked out over the crowd through the window.

That was when he saw Vera.

What the fuck was his ex-wife doing there?

11

Anger rushed through him and he bit back a curse.

Samair must've sensed his abrupt mood change because she stiffened and pulled out of his arms. "Is there a washroom in here?"

He pointed to the far corner and she headed in that direction without looking at him. When she was gone he strode to the little bar, grabbed a cocktail napkin and got rid of the condom. He washed his hands in the bar sink and tamped down his emotions. Up until a minute ago, he'd almost forgotten about his problems.

Samair came back into the room and leaned on the bar top, a sparkle in her eye. "So, Val, what next?"

He blinked.

He loved her straightforwardness. Game playing wasn't anything he was interested in outside the bedroom, and it seemed they were on the same wavelength. "You tell me."

"I haven't decided on my next fantasy yet, but I can tell you one thing: I don't want it to happen in this club again."

He chuckled with her. It was great to be able to talk so openly with a woman. She made him feel almost . . . light-hearted. "You don't like my club?"

"I love your club." She shrugged and her breasts jiggled slightly. He really should've paid more attention to those breasts when he had the chance. "But I can never be— I think I've just decided what my next fantasy is, and I really don't think this is the place for it."

"You going to tell me what it is?"

Little white teeth nibbled on her bottom lip, making him want to run his tongue over it soothingly. She saw where he was looking and her eyes sparkled. "No. I think the surprise should be part of the fantasy. I get to plan it all. You just need to provide a private place for it to happen, and go with it when I begin."

That piqued his interest.

But he really needed to get out on the floor and find out what the hell Vera was doing there. He pulled a business card from his pocket, wrote his private cell phone number on the back, and handed it to her. "Call me when you're ready. I'll make it happen. For now, I need to get back to work."

The light in her eyes dimmed slightly, and he squashed a pang of regret.

God knew he didn't want to cut things short with Samair; if anything, the yen to spend more time with her was growing. But Vera was out in the club and he couldn't let himself get distracted. If his ex-wife was around, trouble was brewing.

"You got it." Samair tucked his card into her tank top and shot him a saucy wink.

They left the private room and he stopped her from walking away with a hand on her elbow. He couldn't help himself. "Next time you wear a skirt like that, don't wear any underwear."

Samair tilted her head up at him and the spark was back in her baby blues. "Ohh, I like that."

He watched her hips swing and her skirt swish as she walked away and blended into the crowd. When he finally tore his eyes from the hypnotizing sight, Vera was standing in front of him.

The bitch always did have radar where he was concerned. There had been a time when he'd thought that meant they were soul mates. Now he knew it just meant she was a manipulative, controlling—

He sucked in a deep breath. He couldn't—he wouldn't let her get to him.

"Vera."

"Valentine. How are you, sweetheart? Playing with one

of your little groupies I see." She flicked her hand in the direction Samair had gone, her voice the bored tone that told him she was deliberately trying to get under his skin. She knew he hated apathy in any form.

"What are you doing here?"

"He never was one for good manners," she said to the poser at her side before giving Val a tight smile. "I thought it was time to show Peter the club since he'll be running it after I buy it."

"It's not for sale."

"But it will be once the bank forecloses." Her painted lips lifted in a victorious smile. "And when it goes up for sale, I'm going to buy it. Peter here is going to run it for me."

"You're counting your eggs before they've hatched, Vera. You never did learn that you can't always have everything you want."

"Pooh." She stepped closer and put a cold hand on his chest. "I think we both know I always get what I want. I got you, didn't I?"

"But you couldn't keep me," he reminded her with a savage pleasure.

Her eyes narrowed and he waited to see if she'd lose her cool. When she didn't respond to his comment he gave her a confident smile of his own. "Risqué will never be for sale; you'd be better off to forget about me and my club and just move on."

She leaned in and for a split second her inner ugliness was clear on her carefully made-up face. "You loved this bar more than you ever loved me, and for that, I'm taking it from you. You never should've walked away from me, Valentine. You're going to regret it."

She swept past him and went up the stairs with her young stud close on her heels. Val's muscles locked and he stayed motionless for several minutes. It wasn't that he couldn't move, but that he didn't want to go back upstairs until he was sure the bitch had left the building.

He hadn't been lying when he'd told Karl that nothing would distract him from his goal. With the money Karl had given him that night, Val now only needed another fifty grand to pay off the mortgage on the building that housed Risqué— and shut down his bitch of an ex-wife's latest effort to hurt him.

He could try to hunt down investors, but it would take time he didn't have. Not to mention the fact that the only person he trusted to invest and not try to take over was Karl.

Karl alone understood just how much Risqué meant to him, and why.

Vera obviously knew it was important, too, or the bitch wouldn't have pulled some strings to get the bank to foreclose three years early in an effort to take it from him. He should've listened to Karl during the divorce. Making it clear that the club was the only thing important to him had backfired.

*   *   *

Whoever the attractive brunette was, Val was not happy to see her. Why that made Samair just a little giddy was something she didn't want to think about too much.

Locked in place, she watched as the seductress sashayed away from Val and up the stairs. She was beautiful, and she moved in a way that said she knew it, and expected all eyes to be on her. Most eyes were on her, but not Val's. Outwardly he looked like he was simply watching the room, but something told Samair he was angry.

Very angry.

Part of her wanted to go to him, to soothe the tension from his shoulders, but the other part of her—the intelligent part—told her to turn on her heel and head for the dancers' booth. Fast.

She'd just gotten away from a life full of complications and entanglements she didn't need. Now was not the time to let herself think that this affair with Val could ever be more than a good time. And good times meant not getting wrapped up in each other's business.

"Sammie!"

Samair's head snapped up as she pushed past the trio of women fawning over Rob. Joey jumped up from her chair and shook her finger at Samair. "Did I just see what I think I saw?"

"Maybe." Heat crept up her neck and Samair fought back a grin. "What do you think you saw?"

Joey grabbed her arm and pulled her away from the table. "Did you just hook up with Val?"

"Uhmm, if by hook up you mean did I just bend over and let him fuck me good, then yes, I hooked up with him."

"Samair!" Joey's jaw dropped. Her expression one of shock and awe with a little bit of dismay thrown in.

"Hang on, I need a drink." She waved at the nearby waitress and ordered a Diet Coke. She felt plenty good all over so there was no need for alcohol. Plus, she had a date for breakfast with her brother the next day. Getting up early for that was going to be hell enough without adding a hangover to it.

The waitress walked away and Samair met Joey's gaze. There was no reason why she shouldn't tell Joey what had happened the first night she was there. The only reason she hadn't told her already was because she'd been so focused on the design thing. Better late than never.

"When I went to thank him for the free drinks last week I sort of propositioned him."

"And he took you up on it tonight?"

"Actually, he took me up on it then." She held up her hand sharply when Joey's mouth opened. "I didn't say anything because we crashed as soon as we got home, and the next day we had other things to talk about. It slipped my mind."

"How the hell could something like that slip your mind?" Joey's voice rose an octave.

"I don't know. My life was kinda turned upside down that night." Samair bit her tongue and tried again—without the sarcasm. "I had other things to think about. Why is this a big deal? It's just sex, and I know you're not a prude."

"Sammie, it's Valentine Ward. Never mind that I work for him, he's . . . well . . . he's got a bit of a reputation."

"For being a player?" He hadn't struck her that way.

"No. As someone you don't want to fuck with." Joey's green eyes were bright with concern. "I've been dancing here for almost three years and I know nothing more about him now than the day I first set foot in here. He's here almost every night, but rumor has it he's connected with the Hells Angels or something."

A biker bad boy. That didn't surprise her. "So? It's not like we're falling in love or anything. It's. Just. Sex."

Very good, very hot, addictive, animalistic sex, but still just sex.

"Just—"

The waitress appeared with Samair's drink and Joey closed her mouth so fast Samair heard her teeth snap together. She paid for her drink, but before either of them could say anything else, Tara and Kelly came racing up to them.

"There you are!"

"We've been looking everywhere for you two!"

Joey rolled her eyes and turned to the newcomers. "What's up?"

"We want outfits, too!" Tara squealed.

"Sammie, will you make us ones, too? Just like Joey's?" Kelly spoke up. "I want mine to be fire-engine red, though."

The two girls continued to spit out questions and instructions like gunfire while Joey pulled Samair into a quick hug. And whispered a soft warning. "I know you can be a bit wild at times, but just be careful with Val, okay? I don't want to see you get hurt."

12

Samair worked her ass off for the next four days.

She drew up designs for the two dancers, went fabric shopping, and began to put the outfits together. Then there were the fittings and the design of Joey's velvet pants, which were giving her fits. Somehow they had to be comfortable and still sexy enough for a cage dancer. Joey would've been happy with a short skirt, but Samair's vision of the outfit included the pants, so she was determined to make it work.

"What about shorts?" Joey asked over the music from where she stood at the breakfast bar, chopping veggies to stow in the fridge.

Life had fallen into a comfortable pattern for them in the

past week. Joey would leave early to spend her days teaching dance classes and either bring home takeout, or cook dinner for them both when she got home. In exchange for Joey taking care of dinner every day, Samair kept the small studio apartment very neat and tidy, and did the dishes every day while Joey was at work. But no matter how clean and neat the place was, it was still extremely crowded with all of Samair's sewing stuff; even more so when Tara and Kelly came by for their fittings.

"Those leather shorts you have would work," Kelly commented as she reached over and snagged a carrot stick.

"Stand still, Kelly." Samair was standing in front of the girl trying to put the finishing touches on the outfit for her.

Joey had put the stereo on and broken out a couple of bottles of wine, and the apartment had taken on a bit of a work-party atmosphere. It was relaxing and comfortable in a way that Samair hadn't felt since she'd last lived with Joey, when they were college roommates.

"Sammie made those for me a few years ago. They've held up really well."

"Yeah, but I see that fringe bra with velvet pants," Samair said. "I can't help it, it's the vision." Maybe she could put a slit up each leg, one that reached above the knee, and decorate them with faux diamonds.

"Oh. My. God!" Tara whipped the bathroom door open and stalked into the room.

"Turn around. Come closer," Kelly ordered from her position on the foot stool. "Damn, that is hot."

"Isn't it awesome?" Tara danced around the room in her new outfit and everyone watched. The material was a faux leather in a rich brown that set off the blonde's coloring.

The long sleeves fitted snug to her arms and the material hugged her body as it cupped her large breasts and buttoned together between them, creating a deep cleavage that drew the eye downward, over her flat tummy to where the tiny miniskirt hung perfectly on her slim hips. The skirt just skimmed the top of her thighs, with a slit over the left one to show a peek of the high-cut velvet panties that covered enough of the dancer's butt to keep things at the delicious tease level.

It was her Latin ballroom–inspired version of a club dancer's outfit. "Joey told me you were a bit of an exhibitionist so I figured that would suit your style and still give you great movement. Think it'll work?"

"It's perfect!" Tara gave her a bear hug. "I can't wait to hit the club tonight. I'm going to give every guy there a hard-on!"

They laughed. Samair tuned out the chatter as she went back to working on the waistband of Kelly's skirt.

Joey turned up the stereo and pointed to Tara. "Give us a dance, girl!"

The small apartment was full of sisterly camaraderie as Tara and Joey danced around amidst the music and jokes.

"Don't move!" Samair steadied the pin in her hand and warned Kelly to stop her eager bouncing. The cut of the skirt waist dipped down very low in front, and if the girl wasn't careful she was going to end up with a new piercing in a very delicate place. Samair put the final pins in place and stepped back.

"Okay, Kelly. Take it off very carefully, and I'll finish it so you can take it home tonight."

"Tonight? It'll be ready tonight?"

"Yup."

When Samair had named the price for custom-made outfits she'd gone high, expecting the girls to barter. But they hadn't blinked. They'd sent the money home with Joey the next night and Samair had been determined to get the outfits perfect and ready for the weekend so they could help spread the word about Trouble.

She sat back and watched Joey and Tara dance as Kelly carefully removed her skirt. They would be her walking, talking, and dancing catalogue.

Things were looking good for Trouble. She'd decided to do the custom orders for the dancers as they came in, and something new for Joey every now and then, but her love was really for lingerie and that was where she wanted to focus.

Kelly handed her the skirt and Samair went to her sewing machine. As she was working on it, she realized she hadn't made herself an outfit in a while. The skirt for Kelly was one she'd like for herself, if she were twenty pounds lighter.

The thought made her pause. She hadn't thought about her weight or her size in almost two weeks. Not since she'd left Kevin.

It had to be because of the phone call from her mother that morning. Judy Jones never actually *nagged* her daughter. That would be tacky. Instead she found other, subtler ways to let Samair know that she was a disappointment.

"Are you eating properly? What about work? Have you found a job yet? Why Joey Kent? I don't know how that girl supports herself. She doesn't even work."

Nothing anyone could say would ever convince her mother that dancing was work. Or that being single and having a few extra pounds wasn't the end of the world but rather something Samair actually *wanted*.

Val hadn't appeared to mind. He'd seemed to really enjoy the plumpness of her curves. So much so that when she was with him, she forgot all about her own problems and imperfections.

"Is it ready?"

Kelly's eager voice broke through Samair's thoughts. She looked at the short Flamenco-inspired black and red skirt still in her hands. "Yes, go try it on."

She laughed as Kelly snatched it out of her hands and dashed into the bathroom. It took all of two minutes for Kelly to change, and the outfit inspired more cheers for Samair. Her chest swelled with pride and for the first time she truly believed that she could have success with her own design label if she worked at it and stayed true to her own vision of things.

Why aren't you dressed?"

Samair glanced up from the sketchbook on her lap. "Huh?"

Whenever Samair sat down with her sketchbook, or in front of the sewing machine, the rest of the world faded into the background and images of sweet, sexy, and even kinky garments took over her brain. It was a good thing when a girl was trying to start a design label, particulary a specialty one like she dreamed of.

After the others had left and while Joey napped, Samair searched the Internet and discovered there weren't any custom lingerie designers in the city. And the ones she had found online were super expensive. She could charge a *lot* for what she wanted to do.

Extremely motivated, she'd started to put down some of the images that had been floating around in her head and hadn't even noticed that Joey was up, let alone showered and almost dressed for the club.

"You're not dressed yet. Hurry up, I need to be at the club by eleven."

Samair sucked her bottom lip between her teeth and looked at Joey. "I wasn't planning on going tonight. I need to come up with some new designs. I've got some great ideas, but I need to get them on paper."

A delicate red eyebrow arched over an eye alight with challenge. "What's wrong? You don't want to see Val?"

"This has nothing do with him." If anything, she wanted to see him very much. Her body was warming and softening in all the right places just thinking about seeing him again. "I don't go to the club with you just to see him. I go because you're there, and it's fun."

"So get off your butt and let's have some fun! It's Saturday night and three, count 'em, *three* of the cage dancers are going to be wearing *your* designs." She snatched the sketchbook out of Samair's hands. "You have to come!"

"I have nothing to wear."

"Bullshit. You have a ton of clothes, and I have a surprise for you that you'll only get if you come out with us. Be sure to wear something of your own, too." By the time she was done talking, Samair was next to the bed, rooting around in the closet they shared.

13

They used the back entrance to the club since Joey was a few minutes late. As soon as they were inside, she disappeared into one of the cages and Samair was left to wander the club floor. She clutched the silver business card holder that Joey had presented to her on the cab ride over and tried not to think about Val.

Not only was the case itself a gift, but it was full of shiny new business cards with Samair's name and cell phone number on them. Samair's throat tightened and she thanked God that she had Joey in her life. A friend who accepted her as she was and encouraged her to chase her dreams. Sweetheart that she was, Joey'd had the cards printed as a gift. Not only that, but the card holder was engraved with one word.

Trouble.

Just knowing that the thing people had always considered her to be was the same thing that was going to make her a success brought forth vital energy from deep within. The pulse-pounding music and atmosphere seeped into her veins and Samair fought the urge to dash into the middle of the dance floor and start handing a card to every person there.

What the hell? Why fight the urge? Trouble was the name, and the crowd *was* her target clientele.

Joey waved at Rob and Tara, who were sharing the main cage, as she climbed into number four. Tara had her new outfit on and was looking hot and sassy next to Rob, who wore only leather pants. His shirtless chest gleamed in the colored strobe lights and she wondered how he could dance all night long in leather pants.

Joey'd done it once, and swore she'd never try again. Sure, she'd made almost three hundred bucks that night, but the pants had chafed so badly, her inner thighs were raw for a week.

Okay, time to switch gears. She closed her eyes and focused on the music. In seconds her blood was humming and she was shaking her ass in time to the frenetic beat. When she danced it was all about feeling. Her mind went blank and thoughts of screaming kids who didn't want to be in a dance class, and the parents that made them attend, floated away on the music.

In her mind she was one with the music; it told her how to move, how to entertain, how to seduce. It told her that everything was going to be all right. All she had to do was believe, and never give up. It told her that one day the dream would be real and she'd be dancing on stage in a movie, in a video, on tour with Beyoncé.

Anything was possible as long as she never gave up.

A tingle of awareness made the hair on her arms stand up and she looked around, spotting a lone man about fifteen feet away who was watching her.

He was dressed in dark gray slacks and a silver button-down dress shirt. Not a typical outfit for the crowd at Risqué, but it suited his slicked-back hair and trimmed goatee. People watched her all the time; she loved it, thrived on it. But this guy's gaze was different. More intense, and slightly creepy. The music changed again, shifting to a medium tempo, sing-along song, and Joey tore her eyes away and focused on the crowd. It was time to get them revved up. If the guy made any sort of move on her, the bouncers would be quick to kick him out on his ass. Harassment wasn't tolerated at Risqué.

She danced and sang and made eye contact with as many people as she could. When the song ended she spun around and found the intense starer at the edge of her cage holding out a business card. She almost ignored him, but his words stopped her in her tracks.

"I'd like to offer you an audition," he called out.

"An audition?" She took the card from his hand. It read Carl Raisen, Raisen Productions, and a phone number.

A producer wanted to offer her an audition? Just like that? She bent down and gave him her best *Don't bullshit me* look. "An audition for what?"

Carl shoved his hands into his pants pockets and rocked back on his heels. "I'm doing a music video for a well-known rock band and I think you'd be perfect for the female part. It's not a huge part, but if you do well, there could be more work in it for you."

Joey wasn't stupid. The world was full of creeps, but stories of supermodels discovered in shopping malls zipped through her head. Maybe, just maybe, this could be the break she'd been waiting for. "What band is it?"

"Give me a call next week to set up an appointment, and if you ace the audition, you can meet the band." He looked her up and down one last time before giving her a wink and walking away.

She stood up slowly, still trying to absorb what had just happened. She folded the card in half and tucked it into her bra, right next to her pounding heart. *Holy shit!*

After searching the crowd, Joey saw Samair on the edge

of the dance floor handing out her business card and pointing to her and Tara and Kelly. The girl was working it. Going
after her dream.

Joey threw her head back and let out a rebel yell. They
were going to make it, the two of them. She just knew it.

o I get one too?"
The husky voice in her ear sent tingles to all of Samair's
pleasure points. She turned away from the girls she'd been
talking to and handed Val one of her new business cards.
"You can have whatever you want, baby."

"Isn't that my line?" His lips curled up on one side.

"You won't share?"

"Don't pout, little girl. If you really want to give me what
I want, I can guarantee it's more than piece of cardboard."

Her temperature kicked up a notch and she pointed to the
phone number on the card. "Just call this number, and I'll see
what I can do for you."

"Custom costumes and lingerie." A dark eyebrow winged
upward. "You're a designer?"

Pride whipped through her. "I am."

He cupped her elbow and led her over to an empty space
in the corner near the bar. "The card only has your name and
phone number. You work for yourself?"

"I do now," she said, casually leaning against the wall. "I

just decided to start my own label last week. The day after I met you, actually."

"Why's that?"

Samair gazed at the man in front of her. He was close to ten years older than her, definitely tough and mature and *über*sexy. And there was real interest in his dark eyes.

"I used to work in a little boutique as a salesgirl while I went to school. It was great because I could take design classes and learn the business side of things from my boss. And at the same time, she let me do alterations for customers to make the clothing better suit their bodies. Everyone was happy." She shrugged and flashed a casual smile. "But . . . things changed and the new boss was a complete control freak. She didn't like me giving honest opinions to the customers, especially if it meant they might buy the less-expensive outfit and shit like that. So I quit."

"And decided to start your own design business." He nodded, his respect clear in his expression.

A big guy wearing a tight black T-shirt with *Risqué* embroidered on the sleeve stopped next to Val and said something to him softly. Samair stepped back and watched them, the music and chatter of the club making it impossible to hear what they were saying. She didn't need to hear them though, the bouncer was pretty hot and the view alone was enough entertainment.

Well built with muscles on his muscles, a nice tan and a

firm round ass, he looked like he should be in the fireman's calendar wearing nothing but a bow. She imagined unwrapping the bow and a little tingle went through her. Damn, she was horny. It was like her body needed to make up for the time she'd spent faking it with Kevin.

Val nodded at the bouncer before stepping forward to focus his attention on Samair again. "Did you make this?" He ran a fingertip along the top edge of her corset, leaving a trail of fire in it's wake.

Breathe, she told herself. No jumping his bones in the middle of the club. "I did." She had to get him up to his office.

"It suits you. Very sensual, but with a tinge of innocence. Do you realize what a turn-on that combination is?"

She licked her lips, struggling to calm her heart rate. He inched closer with every husky word. She shifted with him until her back was flat against the wall and the crowded room disappeared behind his broad shoulders. Things were heating up fast. Again.

She toyed with a button on his dress shirt. The one right above his belt buckle. "What else turns you on?"

"I'd like to—"

"Sammie! Oh my God! You'll never guess what just happened!" Joey ran right up to them and grabbed Samair's arms, dancing around.

Shit! She was never gonna get any at this rate.

Joey glanced at Val, who'd straightened up and taken a step back from the girls. "Sorry to interrupt. But a guy just came up to the cage and asked me to audition for a part in a music video he's producing!"

"Woo hoo!" Samair gave her friend a hug. Joey was practically vibrating with happiness and Samair's heart filled to bursting for her. This was much more important than sex. "This is it, girl. Your big break. Soon you'll be able to tell everyone you were discovered while cage dancing at Club Risqué."

"The guy just approached you while you were dancing in one of the cages?" Val's voice was soft.

"Yeah. I saw him watching for a while, but well, that's the whole point of dancing in those things, right? To get people watching, then moving. Anyway, after a few songs he walked right up and handed me his card. He said to call him to set up an audition if I wanted. Which of course I want!" She rolled her eyes.

Val took the plain white business card from her hand and ran his thumb over the name. "Have you heard of this guy before?"

"No." Joey's grin faltered. "But there're tons of video producers around town. Vancouver's music scene is pretty big."

Samair gave Val a stern look before squeezing Joey's hand. "I'm sure he's for real. Even if it's not a top-forty video, it's work, right? It's getting you out there into the industry where you can make contacts and line up even more jobs."

"Don't mind me," Val said with a self-depreciating chuckle as he handed the card back. "I'm suspicious of everyone. I'm sure it'll be fine. Excuse me for a moment, I'll be right back."

They both watched him walk away.

"Okay, I can see why you hooked up with him. He is *fine*, and if he ever looked at me the way he was looking at you, I'd probably burst into flames."

"Lord help me, that man is seductive."

They looked at each other. "Do you think he's right?"

"About the producer guy?" Samair asked. "I think he's right in that you should be careful, but I also think that you'd be an idiot not to go audition."

A grin split Joey's pretty features. "Good. Because I'm going."

Val returned and directed them to the booth where the dancers usually gathered. There was a bottle of champagne and a tray full of glasses set on the table. "Congratulations, Joey. I hope this is your big break."

After sharing a toast with them, he winked at Samair and disappeared in the crowd.

14

Despair was heavy in Val's gut as he stared at the numbers in front of him.

Three weeks. He had three weeks left to raise fifty thousand dollars. That was over fifteen thousand a week, free and clear of the club's normal running expenses, and he had no way to do it. The account pages he'd printed from his computer weren't giving him any brilliant ideas, but he didn't know where else to look.

His head fell back against the chair and he closed his eyes. He needed an idea. A big one. An event that wouldn't cost him much to put together, but would bring in a large crowd with money to spend.

In his mind he pictured the warehouse when he'd bought

it. It had taken more than money to turn it into the club it was now. Sex sells for sure, but he'd made sure to keep it classy.

He'd worked the club himself every night. Sometimes he worked the bar, sometimes he'd worked the door. Unable to afford to pay dancers, but wanting to keep the cages as a classy feature and not a trashy fixture, he'd gotten the idea to make the cages exclusive only to dancers who passed an audition. In return for dancing for him, he gave them perks like never having to pay the cover, use of the VIP area or private party room for no charge, and occasional bar tabs.

Nothing but pure determination and guts had helped him get Risqué started, and slowly business had picked up. He'd reinvested every penny and kept building and improving the place. And it had paid off.

His club was now one of the hottest in town. He was bringing in a steadily growing income that would make any businessman proud. Only it wasn't enough.

The club would've been his, free and clear, in less than a year at the rate he was going. But it wasn't enough; Vera had to fuck it up. Spoiled little rich girl that she was, she'd taken him leaving her as a sign of war and she was hitting him where it hurt. And it hurt real bad.

What the fuck was he gonna do?

The sharp peal of his cell phone pulled him from his thoughts and he snatched it off the desk. The caller ID read Private Number.

"Hello."

"I'd like to live out another fantasy, please."

Samair.

He eyed the papers spread across his desk. The numbers weren't going to change on their own, and he really shouldn't let himself get distracted.

"Val?"

Maybe a little distraction was just what he needed. Something to rejuvenate his fighting spirit. "You called the right man."

Thirty minutes later the doorbell rang and Val glanced at his watch in surprise. She was on time. He put the un-opened beer in his hand back on the shelf, and closed the fridge.

Sure steps brought him to the front door, and when he opened it his mouth went dry.

With her blond hair tousled, her blue eyes sparkling, and her curves covered up by a shiny black PVC coat, Samair looked like an angel recently kicked out of heaven for misbe-having . . . and glad of it.

The fair skin at her throat sparkled with some sort of glitter, leading his eyes to the shadowed cleavage showcased by the mini trench coat. With the jacket cinched tight at her waist, it flared out to end at mid-thigh and left lots of leg to drool over.

Like the skirt she'd worn the other night, it brought one

thought to his mind: easy access. "Are you wearing panties under that?"

"That's for me to know," she said as she stepped past him to enter the house, "and you to find out."

Her scent filled his head and his body tightened. His dick was waking up fast.

She'd stopped in the middle of the small entranceway and was looking around. The apartment was nothing special, and for the first time since he'd moved in there, he cared what someone thought. When he left Vera, he hadn't really cared where he lived, as long as it was far from his ex. He spent most of his time at the club anyway.

Just when he'd started to think about finding a new place, he found out about the crap Vera had pulled with his bank officer, and he couldn't afford it. When it came to choosing between a nice condo or his club, the club won, hands down. Not that it mattered; Samair wasn't exactly there to help him decorate.

With that in mind he stepped close, invading her personal space as he leaned in, his loose hair falling forward and blending with hers as he whispered in her ear. "I hope to find out more than if you've got underwear on."

He brushed his fingertips against her bare thigh and watched her pupils dilate and the pulse at the base of her throat throb. Good. It was nice to know she was as hot for him as he was for her.

He shifted closer to kiss her, but she braced a hand on the center of his chest and stopped him cold. "Uh-uh."

"No?"

"I'm here to live out a fantasy. A fantasy you promised me." She tilted her head back and met his gaze head on. "In this fantasy, I'm in charge and you're mine to do with as I please."

Christ!

She'd managed to pick the one thing he wasn't sure he could pull off. Control was something he valued way too much to give up to anyone. Yet every muscle in his body was suddenly strung tight, eager to be touched and stroked. His cock was hard enough to hammer nails with and his jeans were tighter than the ball of tension growing in the middle of his chest.

Samair licked her lips, watching him closely.

The urge to say "No way" was strong, but he shoved it away and met her gaze. They weren't strangers anymore, and he wanted to keep it that way. If he said no now, their affair might end right there. And at the moment, she was the only thing giving him pleasure in life. He wasn't ready for it to end.

When he didn't say anything, she dropped her bag on the floor and started a slow stroll around him. Her hand smoothed up over his chest. She fingered the ends of his hair and he suppressed a shiver as goose bumps rose on his skin.

She let go and trailed her hand across his shoulder and down his back.

He waited for her to pat his ass but it didn't happen, and he was surprised at the disappointment he felt.

"You've been deliciously in charge each time we've been together, and it occurred to me that I haven't gotten to play much," she said as she came around in front of him again. "So tonight I'm the kid, and you're the candy store."

Her playfulness helped him relax a little. "Does that mean you're going to eat me?"

"Among other things." She winked and stepped back.

She unbelted the jacket, shrugged it off her shoulders, and it dropped to the floor. She was left standing there in a shiny PVC halter and a matching pair of short shorts.

"You like?" Samair held up her hands and slowly turned in a circle.

Oh yeah. He liked so much he forgot to breathe when he saw that the shorts barely covered her magnificent ass. She was all woman and the caveman inside him was fighting to get out.

"Yes," he growled low in his throat and she laughed.

"Take me to your bedroom."

"Yes, ma'am." He reached around her, grabbed a handful of ass, and lifted. Samair wrapped her legs around his waist and they stared at each other as he walked from the room. Every step had her bumping against his hard-on and he thanked God he lived in such a small place. His bedroom was less than a dozen steps from the front entrance.

He stopped in the middle of his room and arched an eyebrow. "What next, ma'am?"

"You may put me down now." Her full lips twitched. The little minx was trying not to laugh!

He stepped forward and dropped her on the bed, loving the surprised squeak she made when she bounced. She might be playing at being a dominatrix, but they both knew she was doing just that. Playing.

And it was just what he needed. Some good ol', down and dirty, lighthearted fun. Entertainment of the best kind.

Strip for me," Samair commanded from her lounging position in the center of the bed, eager to see Val completely naked for the first time.

Fire flashed in his eyes. The same fire that flared when she'd told him what her fantasy was. As strong and in control as this man always was, it was obvious that the thought of letting her have free rein with his body turned him on.

She'd known it was a risk to try this with him. But he was always so in control when they were together. Each time he had her so hot and horny that she wasn't even aware she hadn't gotten to touch him until it was all over.

The idea of taking charge had come to her when they

were still in the private room at Risqué. He had just given her an orgasm so fucking strong her knees had buckled, and she'd still wanted to lay him down and climb on top.

Now she was gonna make it happen, and she was going to take her time doing it.

Val stood at the foot of the bed, hands on his hips. When he'd opened the door for her and she'd seen him with his hair down for the first time, her fingers had immediately started itching to stroke the glossy blue-black strands. Now she wanted to see it against bare skin.

He reached over his head and pulled the faded blue T-shirt off in one smooth move. She drank in her first sight of his naked chest. She'd felt those muscles under her hands, against her body, but she'd yet to see them. His chest was firm, with little brown nipples poking through a small pelt of dark hair. The washboard hardness of his stomach made her mouth water. Her gaze followed the treasure trail of hair from his belly button to where it disappeared under his waistband.

His hands paused on the last button of his button-fly jeans and she raised her gaze to his.

"Spread your legs for me." His voice was husky, raw.

She realized her own hand was between her thighs, mirroring his actions. She let her knees fall apart and ran a fingertip over her covered slit and up to the bare skin of her belly.

"I want you naked, Val. Hurry up."

"Yes, ma'am." He shoved his jeans over his hips, taking any underwear he'd had on with them. She was pleased to see that he made a point of taking his socks off, too.

She sat up and inched her way to the end of the bed.

"Come closer," she commanded when she was sitting with her feet on the floor.

She'd planned to tease them both once he was naked. But the sight of his long, thick cock standing so proud was too hard to resist. She reached out, cupped his ass, and pulled him closer. Rubbing her cheek over the silk covered hardness, she inhaled his scent and let her breath tease him.

His butt clenched under her hands and she scraped her nails across them lightly, eliciting a low groan from him. With slow, deliberate moves she kissed the flat of his belly and the crease of his thigh. Then when his hands reached for her head, she took him in her mouth.

She parted her lips and took him as deep as she could. Gentleness and teasing gone, she licked and sucked with more enthusiasm than skill. He felt so good in her mouth, his thighs trembling under her hands. He tasted of musky male and pure sex.

Sucking air in through her nose, she fought to breathe as she bobbed her head up and down. With each stroke she swirled her tongue around the shaft, feeling it throb and grow harder and thicker in her mouth as his hands clenched in her hair and his moans filled the room.

She was in control. She was making him moan and sigh and cry out her name. She didn't want it to stop.

Reaching between his thighs with one hand, she palmed his heavy sac. Rolling his balls between her fingers, she squeezed lightly.

His fists tightened in her hair. "Christ, you're gonna kill me, darlin'."

Heart pounding, blood racing through her veins, Samair pulled her mouth away and looked up at him. He gently stroked a finger down her cheek and the air between them shifted. At that moment, they didn't need words to communicate.

Samair reached for his hands and lay back on the bed, pulling him down above her. The playful teasing atmosphere was gone, as was her desperate hunger for him. In it's place was a connection to him like she'd never felt before.

The full length of his body came down on top of her and she reveled in his weight. Eyes still locked on hers, he lowered his head and touched her lips softly, a light grazing back and forth before she parted them and his tongue slipped inside.

Lips softened, tongues rubbed, and heartbeats matched as they looked deep into each other's eyes. Passion, trust, and acceptance were silently given and received.

Samair's hands ran over Val's back, the muscles rippling beneath her palms. His chest pressed down on hers, his hips flexing between her thighs making her insides ache to be filled. Bracing her hands on his shoulders, she arched up and rolled them both so she was on top. With a quick wiggle she got rid of her shorts before straddling Val's hips and taking him deep inside her.

"Yes," Samair hissed.

Val's mouth opened, but no sound came out.

"Oh, Val," she murmured as she began to rock her hips. "This is going to be so good."

His heavy-lidded gaze fueled her inner fire in a way that his hands on her hips couldn't. There was lust and fire and raw hunger in his gaze as he watched her. His fingers dug into the softness of her hips for a moment, then those hot hands reached back and cupped her ass. He squeezed and fondled her plumpness and she'd never felt more beautiful or sexy in her life.

Straightening up, she watched him watch her as she ran her hands over her belly and rib cage. She slid the halter up and cupped her bared breasts. When she pinched her nipples, her insides clenched in response. Val groaned and thrust upward, going deeper.

She smiled, and did it again.

Unable to tease herself anymore, she braced her hands on his chest, looked deep into his eyes, and started to ride him. She lifted and lowered onto the man who had lit the fire within her, her speed picking up as the bed squeaked and bounced and she slammed down onto him. His hands gripped her ass as he matched her thrust for thrust, his panting mingling with hers to make erotic music.

"Samair . . . come on, baby . . . I'm going to come."

She closed her eyes, focused on the feel of his naked cock deep inside her. Touching her core. Touching her heart.

Her pussy tightened and his cock jerked at the same moment his thumb slid between them and circled her clit.

"Yes!"

Warmth filled her pussy and tremors shook her body as she ground down on Val and welcomed the pleasure of taking everything he had to give.

15

She lay curled up against Val's side, her hand over his heart. It slowed to a steady thump-thump as she struggled to get her own breath back. What had started out as a playfully naughty fantasy had somehow turned into intense, emotional . . . *lovemaking*.

With a man she barely knew.

Yet, that connection . . . the wordless communication . . . She hadn't imagined it, had she?

There had been a moment when promises and assurances had been given. They were safe, they trusted each other. With their bodies anyway. She was not ready to let her heart get involved.

Samair closed her eyes and took a deep breath. "Wow," she whispered.

His chest shook and she lifted her head. He was laughing? She smacked his chest. "You laughing at me?"

"Not *at* you, babe. With you." He slid from the bed and, brow furrowed, ran a hand through his hair. "That little scene took a bit of an unexpected turn on us, didn't it?"

"Yeah."

She tore her gaze away from his still-naked body. She had to get this back under control; a relationship was not what she was looking for.

No way, no how. She'd just started to get a foothold on what she really wanted from life, she wasn't going to slide back into the pattern of what was the *expected* thing to do.

"Listen, Val." She hesitated, chewing on her lip for a moment. Hell, she had to say it. "I know that was sort of intense, but I'm not really looking for anything serious. This 'living out my fantasies' thing is about as much as I can handle in my life right now."

His full lips tilted into a slow sensual smile and his shoulders relaxed. "That works perfectly for me."

"Really?"

"Yeah, I've got a few things going on in my own life right now, and to be honest, you and our little sexcapades are about all I can deal with as well."

Sexcapades.

Fun, sexual adventure with a hot man. Just what she'd wanted, right?

"So this"—she waved a hand back and forth between them—"casual lover arrangement works for you? We each have our separate lives, but get together when we want. No strings, no ties?"

He winked at her. "I wouldn't say no ties. I've suddenly developed a bondage fantasy or two of my own."

"Really?" She laughed when he crawled back onto the bed and prowled toward her. "That's good, because I've yet to have my way with you. On your back."

He froze mid-prowl. "That wasn't what I was thinking of."

"But it's what I'm thinking of, and you said you'd make *my* fantasies come true." She sat up on her knees and flashed him a wicked smile.

That lovely energy was swelling inside her again. The one that made her feel as if she were the sexiest thing on earth, and nothing could stop her from getting what she wanted. And right now she wanted to play with Val.

With an exaggerated sigh he flopped onto his back, arms flung wide. "Be gentle with me, please."

The words were lighthearted, but in that moment Samair realized just how hard it was for him to give up control.

Desire had flashed hot and fast in his eyes when she'd first told him her fantasy, but his body had been super tense. Now he didn't seem tense, but he did look . . . resigned.

And that just would not do.

She adjusted her plan. "Why don't we start with a shower?"

He lifted his head and stared at her. "Okay. You're the boss."

"I'll be right back." She made a quick dash to the living room to grab the bag she'd dropped when she'd first come in. Val's ability to make her brain fog over with a look had made her forget all about her plan almost as soon as she'd walked in the place.

But not anymore.

She dropped the bag on the edge of the bed, struggled out of the fitted halter, and followed him into the bathroom. Once the shower spray was on, she stepped into the tub first. The spray was hot and felt wonderful. Just the thing.

Val stepped in behind her and held out a bar of soap. Turning so he received the majority of the spray, she grinned. "It's my turn to play," she said.

Starting with his chest, she began to wash him. He kept his hands by his sides while she lathered up his pecs, running her fingers through the soft pelt that covered his muscles. She fingered his nipples, circling them, tweaking them until they were rock hard. She ran her hands lower down his body and leaned forward to place her lips on his neck.

His hands rested lightly on her hips, not pushing her away or holding her close. Just . . . touching. She handed him the soap and started to rinse him off, nibbling and lick-ing at his neck and shoulders once the soap dissipated. She worked her way down to his chest with her lips, sucked one nipple into her mouth, and his whole body jerked in reaction.

Delighted, she pulled back and focused on the other one.

Her hands floated over his belly to his groin. She cupped his semi-hard cock and delighted in the feel of it slowly growing again as she fondled him. When he was almost fully hard, she pulled back. "Turn around."

He quirked an eyebrow at her but did as she requested. She positioned them so he stood under the spray. It landed on his chest and she was behind him. She lathered up her hands again and handed the soap to him. "Hang on to this please." Then she went to work on his back and shoulders.

Soapy water sluiced downward and her gaze followed it to his fabulous ass. Firm and tight and rounded just perfectly, it was better than she ever thought when imagining it under his clothes. She ran her hands over his butt cheeks, pulling them apart and then squeezing them together again. Unable to resist, she bent low and bit him. He jumped, a small groan escaping.

She straightened up and brushed her hands over the tops of his shoulders to reach his collarbone, then over and down farther in front, skimming the top of his pecs. Unable to tease herself or him anymore, she pulled her hands back and slid them around under his arms to run across his flat belly. She pressed the length of her naked body against his backside and kissed his shoulder.

His heart pounded under her hand as she nudged his hair out of the way and nibbled on his neck. She tweaked his nipples the same way she liked to play with her own. They hardened instantly and he sighed in approval. One hand remained on his chest and the other slid down his flat stomach to play with the wiry curls surrounding the base of his cock. His breathing picked up and he widened his stance, bracing himself.

She ran her right hand gently over his engorged cock and pulled it away from his belly then used a fingertip to spread the juice oozing from the tip. A moan escaped his lips when she reached down and cupped his heavy balls in her left hand.

"Feel good?" she whispered in his ear. "Feels great to me. All hard steel wrapped in velvet. I can feel your blood pumping into your cock. It's still growing in my hand. You're almost too big for me to grip."

She pressed her breasts into his back, urging him to lean against her. To give in to her, to the pleasure. "Is that how it feels when you touch yourself? Do you think of me when you jack off? I want you to after this. I want you to remember how it feels when it's my hand pumping your cock and massaging your balls."

Val dropped the soap and reached back to grip her hips and pull her tighter against him. Knowing she finally had control over this powerful masculine body gave her an incredible rush as she gripped his hard-on firmly and pumped her fist faster.

She'd never played with a man like this before. It brought a level of intimacy she hadn't anticipated, but welcomed. Her sex throbbed between her thighs, but the real pleasure she was feeling was due to the sounds escaping from Val. She spread around the pre-come leaking steadily from the tip to ease the friction and added a twist to her wrist. A shiver ran through him when her fingers brushed over the sensitive head.

The harsh sound of his breathing was only one signal of how close he was to coming. His balls tightened and crawled closer to his body, so she pulled her hand away from them and brought it back up to pinch a distended nipple.

"Come for me," she whispered in his ear as his fingers gripped her thighs. "You're so hard, so thick. I want to feel you come. Give it to me, baby. Give me your come."

His chest shook and a guttural groan bounced off the walls of the steamy bathroom as his hips thrust forward against her hand and hotness surged from his throbbing cock.

She held him gently in the palm of her hand until his breathing slowed to normal. Then she urged him to turn in her arms. She pressed kisses along his jaw until she reached his mouth. After a soft meeting of their lips, she backed away and reached for the shampoo.

Val leaned against the tile wall and watched her with slumberous eyes as she washed.

Finally, unable to stand the silence anymore, she grinned and flicked water in his face. "Did I tire you out, old man?"

16

Val snorted and smacked her on the ass. Old man indeed. He may be ten years older than her, but she made him feel like a horny seventeen-year-old again. That wasn't all she was making him feel, but it was all he was prepared to deal with.

With a quick jerk on the faucet, he shut off the water and lifted her out of the tub, the shampoo falling from her hand to the shower floor. She wanted to play? He was ready to play.

"Let me," he said when she grabbed one of the towels he'd set out. He pulled it from her hand and dried her off with slow, gentle pats.

After squeezing the excess moisture from her hair, he gave himself a quick pat-down and ushered her into the bedroom.

There was a black bag at the foot of his bed and he remembered her dropping it in the hallway when she'd called him her "candy store."

"What's in there?" He'd bet money it was sex toys. His little playmate was nothing if not adventurous.

"That's for me to know and you to find out when I want you to." She flashed a devilish grin and pointed to the bed. "Now, on your back, hands behind your head."

"Didn't we try this already?"

"Yes, but I got distracted. Now be quiet or I'll have to gag you."

He swallowed a chuckle and stretched out on the mattress. This was going to be more fun than he'd ever imagined.

Samair pulled a piece of black silk out of the bag and leaned over him. His heart raced and his chest got tight when she covered his eyes and tied the material behind his head. "They say when you lose one sense, all of the other senses get sharper."

They were right. His groin tightened as he breathed in her clean scent, and the hair on his arms stood up at her closeness. She wasn't touching him yet, but he could *feel* her, sense her. Then her mouth was on his. Nothing else touched, but tongues tangled and breath mingled, making his pulse skip.

Sliding her lips across his jaw and under his chin, she nibbled her way down his neck to his collarbone, and then continued to his chest. He'd never realized just how sensitive his nipples were. She licked and bit at them, brushing her own against his belly, and he had to fist his hands to keep from grabbing her. The urge to throw her on her back and conduct some explorations of his own was a strong one.

But even stronger was the urge to give this woman another of her fantasies.

She wiggled her hips and shimmied her body slowly down his until his hard-on nestled between her breasts. Her weight shifted again, and soon her whole body dragged along the length of his. Christ, his blood pressure was picking up fast, and his dick was demanding attention. He couldn't believe his body was still so damn eager after two monstrous orgasms in the last hour.

The woman was magic.

A soft ripping sound reached his ears and then a gentle hum. Before he could worry about what she was going to do with a vibrator, she touched his nipple with it and a shock went through his body and straight to his dick.

Samair's delighted laugh washed over him and he did his best to lie still for her while she circled one nipple, then the other. "It's a little purse-sized neck massager," she said as she moved it over his collarbone and up to the soft spot behind his ear. He twitched and jerked his head away with a growl.

"Ohhh, you're sensitive there, huh? Let's see where else your hot spots are."

His hands twitched and he laced them firmly together. "I could show you where they are."

"No. I want to find them on my own. Much more fun."

Every hair on his body stood on end as she trailed the toy over his shoulder and down his rib cage. When she moved it over the crease of his thigh, his body jerked again and a moan escaped.

"Ohh, another hot spot."

Then she dipped her hand between his thighs and cupped his balls. The vibrations ripped through him and he shot up, grabbed her shoulders, and flipped her onto her back.

Her soft body cushioned his and he found her mouth. Plunging his tongue between her lips, he pinned her body to the mattress with his own. Her fingers speared into his hair and her legs wrapped around his hips as he thrust home.

She tugged his head up by his hair and he gasped.

"Stop!" Her chest was rising and falling beneath him; her pussy was hot and wet and clenching hungrily at his cock. It took every ounce of willpower he had to freeze.

"Samair?"

Her hips rolled and he went a little deeper. "Wait," she said.

"I am waiting, babe. You moved that time." He sucked oxygen deep into his lungs and felt a trickle of sweat run down his cheek. He lifted a hand to take off the blindfold, but her hand on his stopped him.

"Keep the blindfold on, and do as I say. I'm still in charge."

He could live with that.

He planted his hands on the mattress and rotated his hips. Her cunt spasmed and his cock throbbed. He pulled out, and sunk back in. She was so soft, so warm and slick. In . . . out. In . . . out. He established a slow, steady rhythm.

"Oh yes," she sighed. "That's it. No coming until I say so."

"You're the boss."

It was fine by him; now that he was inside her, he could last forever.

The gentle hum warned him a split second before she put the thing to his nipple again. Pleasure whipped through him, a groan escaped, and he thrust deeper, harder.

"My, my; you are sensitive, aren't you?" Samair's voice held a note of awe that stroked his insides. "I can feel your cock jerk inside me when I do this."

He ran a nightclub, women hit on him fairly often, and he had certainly heard dirty talk before. But for some reason, hearing it come from Samair made it so much more potent. She scraped the nails of one hand down his back while the other played the vibe over his nipple, and he concentrated on not coming as he worked his hips. He shifted his weight, angled in a little differently, and heard her gasp.

He picked up speed with each stroke, going deeper, faster,

harder. "Yes, that's it," she urged. A muffled thump and both of her hands on his back told him she'd gotten rid of the vibe.

"Closer, come down to me." She pulled at him until he bent his elbows and her mouth was on his nipples.

He groaned as she went from one to the other, nibbling and sucking at him. Her hands traveled down his back and over his ass. Her nails dug in for minute, then a sharp slap landed on one ass check. "Faster, Val. Harder. Make me come."

Gritting his teeth, he buried his face in her neck and pumped his hips. Her scent filled his head; her words echoed in his ears and she bit his chest, muffling her scream as her body tensed and her cunt clamped down on him. Wet warmth massaged his cock and he let himself go, his own shout of satisfaction mixing with hers.

Val knew he should move. Roll off of Samair. But he didn't. He just lay there, most of his weight on his elbows, with his head buried in her neck and his body covering hers.

He wasn't aware of how much time passed before she wiggled beneath him, but he took the hint and rolled to his back, keeping her with him as he drifted off to sleep.

17

Val stood in his office and stared at the crowded floor below him. The dance floor was packed, the bartenders were keeping the liquor moving at a steady flow, and there was a line at the door.

God, he loved Risqué. He loved the atmosphere, the music, and the crowd. He loved that it was a place where people went to have a good time, to let loose and forget their troubles.

Most of all he loved that it gave him a place where he belonged. It was his home. And if he didn't take a chance, he was going to lose it.

"Business is great," he said in reply to Karl's question. "But it's not enough. I need to do something. One big *some-*

thing to make a big lump sum of money so that paying off the loan doesn't bankrupt me. What good is paying off the fucking loan if I can't afford to keep the place open?"

"Not much good at all, brother."

Val kept his back to his friend, and went for it. "If I hold an exclusive lingerie and fetish wear fashion show at the club, do you think you can get some of the crowd from the Dungeon to show up?" He turned away from the view and waited for Karl's answer.

"Possibly. Depends on when you hold it, and how exclusive it is."

"It could be an invitation-only event."

Karl straightened up on the couch, taking more interest in the idea. "A lot of the people who would be willing to spend serious money on that sort of stuff prefer to stay anonymous. They might not be comfortable in an open bar."

Val thought about it. "I could set it up for private bidding or purchasing on the products. Use the bachelor room for a small, more private showing for select individuals."

"That would probably work. When are you thinking of doing it?"

"I haven't set a date yet." Or mentioned the idea to Samair.

She was gone from his bed when he woke up on Monday morning and he hadn't seen or heard from her since. He should be happy that she was sticking to her word, keeping things casual.

He *was* happy about it. It was everything else in his life that was fucked up. But not for long.

"I'd do it soon though. If I work it right, this could be the way to meet that final payment."

"About that." Karl sat forward and rested his elbows on his knees. "I talked to my bank guy and liquidated some funds, so if you need it, I'll have a fair amount of cash handy in a couple of weeks."

Stunned, Val just stared at him. Karl had plans for his money, his own dreams.

"Consider it a personal loan, not an investment. This is just to shut that bitch down and make sure the club is and always will be yours."

He didn't know what to say. "Buddy—"

"Look," Karl cut him off. "I feel like this is partly my fault for not making sure your ass was covered six ways from Sunday in that divorce."

"That's bullshit, man. You did everything I asked you to." Anger rose in his chest. "It's not your fault, or mine, that we never considered Vera's using her family connections to pull strings at the bank. It's fucking devious of her, and there was no predicting it."

"Still—"

"Still, nothing. This fetish fashion thing will work out. I managed to build this club up from an abandoned warehouse, I can fucking throw a party big enough to raise some money."

All he needed was a hot theme, which he had, and he was off. "If—*when* this fashion show event idea plays out . . . I won't have any worries."

"Where'd the idea come from anyway?"

Samair's naughty PVC outfit. Her adventurous streak. Her fantasy list.

"Sex sells, and I need something that will sell fast and furious." He met Karl's probing gaze head on. "Plus, I met a woman with a bit of a thing for interesting lingerie recently. It got me thinking."

"A woman, huh?"

He waited; he knew what was coming next. Karl was getting too predictable in his cynicism. "Would this be the curvy blond plaything from a week or two back? The one you said was entertainment, not a distraction?"

"Yes. And I was right, she's not a distraction. In fact, she's been . . . inspirational."

That got a wolfish grin. "Yeah?"

"Definitely."

18

Samair dashed across the small apartment, dripping water and cursing as she dove for the ringing phone on the bed. She was in the shower when it started ringing, and normally she'd leave it, but she'd actually started to get some calls in response to the cards all the dancers were handing out, and she wasn't taking a chance on missing an order.

"Samair speaking," she said breathlessly.

The first time a call came in from a client there'd been a misunderstanding when Samair had just answered with hello. After saying it was the wrong number, they hung up and called back, then asked if they'd reached Trouble Designs. But answering the phone by saying Trouble also hadn't gone over so well when her mother had called.

"Samair, it's Val."

Warmth swept through her at the sound of his deep voice. "Hi, Val, How are you doing today?"

"Good. Listen, I have a proposition for you. Can I drop by your office in a couple of hours?"

Her office? She looked around the small apartment. Her sewing machine was set up on the kitchen table, the half dressed sewing dummy was blocking the television, and bolts of fabric were stacked up along the far wall. "Umm, sure. I work out of the apartment right now, so you can come by anytime."

She gave him the address and they hung up. Flopping over on the bed she wondered what to wear for his visit. She was intrigued by the idea of him having a proposition for her that wasn't covered in the casual lover arrangement they'd made.

By the time the buzzer for the security door downstairs rang a couple of hours later, Samair had dressed in a casual pair of jeans and a knit T-shirt and cleaned up the apartment. It was still small and crowded, but there was really no way around that. She buzzed him up and concentrated on some deep breathing. Just knowing she was going to see him had her body readying itself for a good time.

She swung open the door and tried not to drool at the sight coming up the stairs.

Black leather covered him from head to toe. A straight-fit

jacket hung open from his broad shoulders to his trim waist, and heavy chaps covered him from the waist to ankle. Heavy boots completed the look.

She'd never found boots so sexy before.

"You look hungry, little girl," said the big bad wolf when he was directly in front of her.

She tilted her head back and met his heated gaze. "Oh, yeah."

Humor and heat combined to make his eyes swirl like melted chocolate. His mouth lifted at one corner and he brushed against her slowly as he stepped into the apartment.

Oh, Lord. She eyed the way the leather of the chaps framed his perfect denim-covered ass and swallowed a moan. She was in trouble.

He set the little skullcap he carried down on the island counter that separated the kitchen from the rest of the unit, then turned and looked back at her. "Are you coming in?"

She nodded her head and grinned at him before shutting the door. "Sorry. I had to take a minute to drool over your ass."

His laugh filled the room as he shook his head. "You're something else, you know?"

"I'm going to take that as a compliment." She sauntered past him and perched on a kitchen stool.

"It was meant as one."

She reached out, slipped her fingers under his leather belt, and tugged him closer. Only he resisted.

He grabbed her wrist and pulled her hand away from his belt. "I have a proposition for you."

"I have one for you, too." She winked and reached for him again.

"Not that kind of proposition." He stepped out of her reach and deeper into the living area.

When had she developed a leather fetish? All she could think about while Val checked out the space was how hot he would look with his hair down and no jacket, no shirt, and those yummy leather chaps. They might be perfect for riding a Harley, but they really made her want to stretch out spread-eagle on any surface and scream "Ride me!"

All he'd have to do was unzip his pants.

Her insides heated and her nipples hardened to the point of pain while she imagined the feel of that worn leather rubbing against her inner thighs, her hands smoothing over it to get to his perfect ass and clutching him to her while he pumped away.

"It's about your designing."

Her spine snapped straight. Huh? "What about my designing?"

He'd stopped in front of the sewing dummy and was fingering the stretch lace teddy she'd been pinning together. He gave her a look that said he knew where her mind had been before continuing. "Did you get any bites from the cards you handed out at the club last week?"

"A couple."

"Would you be interested in doing a show of your work at the club?"

"Like a fashion show?"

He planted his hands on his hips and gazed at her steadily. "Yeah."

A fashion show at Risqué? What a freaking fabulous idea!

"I'd love to!" She jumped off the stool and rushed at him, talking a mile a minute. "I have some great ideas for more dancer's outfits, and even some Goth style—"

"Not a clothing show," he said quickly, cutting her off. "A lingerie one. In particular—fetish wear. Sort of like the PVC outfit you wore to my place the other day. You could have some of the softer stuff, but, mainly, the kinkier the better."

Something wasn't right. It just seemed too easy to have the opportunity to showcase her brand-new business at one of the hottest clubs in town. "Why are you doing this?"

"Your outfit inspired me the other day. You made it, right?" She nodded and he took off his jacket before dropping onto the loveseat. He lounged back against the corner and looked up at her with an unreadable expression. "I think you're good at what you do, and this could be a good thing for us both."

"Exactly how is it good for you? There's something you're not telling me and I need you to be honest with me."

"Sit." He patted the cushion next to him.

She settled onto the loveseat and waited. When he leaned forward, the scent of man and leather tickled her nose and she desperately tried to not think about having the bad boy biker tie her up and lick her all over.

Val's gut clenched. He couldn't do it. He couldn't tell Samaii what she wanted to hear. He'd opened up to a woman once before, and that was what had gotten him into this predicament in the first place.

He looked into her soft baby blues and steeled himself. "It's a business proposition, that's all. I'll provide the place and the promotions, you provide the product and the models, and we both make some money."

The wheels were turning in her head; he could almost see them. She was smart. She knew there was more to it than what he's said, but she was also thinking about how good it would be for her. He liked that.

"When will the show be?"

"Next weekend. That's ten days to get it all set up, plenty of time."

"Ten days! I need longer than that to design a whole line of lingerie. Especially a specialized line like you mentioned." Her cheeks pinkened. "I don't know anything about fetish wear, really."

Blood rushed south and his cock swelled. Her blush made him want to do dirty things to her. "I have to work tonight, but if you meet me at Risqué around midnight, I can take you to one of the underground clubs for a bit. You can see what sort of outfits people in the lifestyle wear and what they like. As for *knowing* the stuff, I want your take on it, not anyone else's. Like the bra and shorts you wore the other day. Very simple for fetish wear, but damn hot, and not like the stuff I've seen before. It has to be unique to sell for the prices we're going to set."

Her eyes brightened. "The stuff you've seen before?"

He chuckled. His little wild child was getting hot. "I've been to the club before. Although it's really not my thing, I'm sure you'll see some outfits that will . . . inspire you."

A naughty smile lifted her lips as she crawled across the small space between them and straddled his lap. "I see something that inspires me right now."

She lowered her head and slanted her mouth across his. Her little tongue probed and he parted his lips, letting her invade. The scent of pure woman filled his head and Samair's unique flavor caused him to clutch her hips and pull her closer.

One hand cupped her ass while the other slid up her rib cage and found a soft, plump breast topped with a cherry-hard nipple.

He moaned, tearing his mouth away from hers to bury it in her neck. He nibbled and licked at the taut, exposed skin and reached for the hem of her T-shirt.

"Can I join in?"

Samair tensed in his arms and his movements stalled.

"Hey, Joey," Samair said huskily, looking over Val's shoulder with heavy-lidded eyes.

He couldn't see the newcomer, but he could feel her presence close behind him, and the look in Samair's eyes wasn't telling him anything. Was she into threesomes? Shit, was she into women? He'd seen the two girls dance together, but women teased and taunted on the dance floor all the time so he'd thought nothing of it.

There was a rustling noise behind him. Joey.

"Val?" Samair said softly.

He gave a small shake of his head and smacked her on the ass. "This was supposed to be a business stop only. If I'm going to take you to the Dungeon tonight, I have to go do some work now. Maybe another time."

She slid off his lap and he stood to leave. He'd had a few threesomes before, and they weren't that great. Sure it was hot to watch two women make out, but when naked, he preferred one woman, focused completely on him.

*　　*　　*

Samair watched Val say good-bye to Joey and saunter out the door. The minute the door closed Joey turned to her with a giggle. "Who'd have thought the offer for a threesome would scare that man away?"

Samair waved her hand. She didn't think the idea of a threesome scared Val. She didn't think the idea of *anything* scared Val. He'd come by with a business proposition, and that was what had happened.

"Oh, oh! Guess why he was here."

Joey wiped the corner of her mouth with a fingertip. "Sorry, gotta wipe the drool off. You two were so fucking hot, I'm on fire from just watching you."

Samair fought a blush, which was silly because it wasn't like Joey had never seen her have sex before. A threesome in college was what had started their own short-lived affair. She waved away the thoughts of sex . "He asked me to put on a lingerie show at Risqué!"

Joey's jaw dropped.

Samair grabbed her by the arms and started jumping up and down. She couldn't contain herself any longer.

"A show, Joey. In the club. He said it'll be a private event, like an auction. He'll do all the promotions and bring in the buyers. All I have to do is supply the lingerie and the models." She stopped dead. "You'll model for me, right? You and

Tara and Kelly? Will Jason and Rob be into it, too? I might need a couple more, too, the five of you might not be enough. I have to get busy. I need more outfits."

Her brain was zipping along at a mile a minute. So much to think about, so much to do.

"Of course we'll model for you. This is gonna be awesome. Trouble will rock the club!"

Samair spun around on her heel. "I need to raid your closet. Have you ever heard of the Dungeon? I'm supposed to go there tonight with Val."

"the Dungeon?" Joey followed her into the bed area. "Sammie, honey, that's a sex club."

Clothing thoughts fled and images of couples in all sorts of positions filled her head. Her tummy clenched and her sex throbbed. "Really?"

"Yeah. I never knew you were so into kink. Although that certainly explains the dangerous air around Valentine. And why there's never any gossip about him and women around the club." She tilted her head a little, her eyes wide with laughter and intrigue. "Why didn't you tell me he was a fetish freak? What's your fetish? Sammie, you *have* changed."

Samair smacked her on the arm and laughed. "I don't have any fetishes. Shit, I barely even know what fetishes are." Panic hit. "Joey. Talk to me. I don't want to look like a complete innocent tonight."

"Honey, a complete innocent doesn't bend over and

let a guy she barely knows fuck her in the back room of a nightclub."

She wouldn't blindfold him and search out all his erogenous zones either. She'd been living by the seat of her pants for almost two weeks, and she'd never been so happy. Things were going well. She just needed to keep moving forward.

No fear.

19

After going through her closet with Sammie and napping for a few hours, Joey was full of energy. She was also determined to get laid. She'd interrupted Val and Sammie twice now, and the pheromones the couple exuded whenever they were close more than reminded her just how long it'd been since she'd had any action.

"If I don't come home tonight, don't worry, okay?" Joey said as she stepped out of the cab.

Sammie shut the cab door and turned to her. She gestured to her long black pencil skirt and short PVC coat that was belted to hide the boned leather corset she'd borrowed. Sammie's boobs were a cup size bigger than Joey's, and she was feeling a bit shy about the way she spilled over the top, but she was trying to hide her nerves. "Looking like this, I'm thinking I might not make it home tonight, myself."

They high-fived and sashayed past the line outside the club. When Joey saw the big blond just inside the door, her pulse jumped and something fluttered in her stomach.

"Hi, Mike." Playing the part, Joey trailed her fingertip across the bouncer's muscled chest. "Is it going to be a good night?"

Mike Davis was a fairly new addition to the security staff at the club, and had been her secret crush for the past six months. The first time she'd seen him was the first time she'd ever been speechless in front of a man.

He was a constant flirt. His close-cropped blond hair and baby face gave him a boy-next-door look, but the twinkle in his green eyes said he had a bit of the devil in him. The right kind of devil.

"It's always a good night when you're dancing, Joey," he said with a wink.

"You gonna put that boy out of his misery tonight?" Sammie asked after they were inside the club.

They stopped for a minute at the rail overlooking the lower floor. Joey tried not to stare at Mike where he stood twenty feet away. The dark suit jacket he wore over his T-shirt fell smoothly from his broad shoulders and looked real nice, but it hid his butt. She wanted to see that butt, amongst other things. "Yeah, I think it's time to go for it."

"I don't get why you haven't gone for it before," Samair said.

She shrugged.

"Uh-uh." Sammie stepped in front of her and looked her in the eye. "You don't get to just shrug it off with me. Spill it, Joey."

"Spill what?"

But there was no fooling her. "You're never shy with guys, so what's so special about him?"

"He's so . . . God, it sounds so stupid." She realized she was twisting her ring around on her finger, a sure sign of nerves. "He's just so *nice*."

Sammie laughed. "Nice is a good thing, Joey."

Heat crept up her neck and she cursed the gene that gave her red hair and fair skin. "I know nice is good, but I don't have much experience with nice guys. And as much as he flirts with me, he's never asked me out. Shit, I've never seen him take any girl home from work. Maybe he's gay."

Sammie turned and looked him over again. "He doesn't look gay to me."

She didn't really believe he was gay either. Nope, no way was that man gay. He had way too much testosterone. However, there was no denying he was a nice guy . . . and she'd always been a bad girl. He'd probably never be interested in a girl like her—a dancer. But he was a man, and there were few men who would turn her down if she offered them a no-strings night of lovin'. She'd wanted him since she first saw him, and she was going to have him.

"I'll go flirt with him later. I'd better get down on the floor first."

"Joey."

"What?" She met Sammie's gaze and felt her blush return. She couldn't hide anything! *Damn it!*

"Don't be a chicken shit. Go talk to him now. Make a date for after work."

"I have to teach tomorrow. Maybe tonight isn't a good night after all."

Samair frowned. "Joey."

Jesus! What was wrong with her? She'd been hot for Mike for six months and she wanted to get laid. What was the big deal? "Fine. Whatever. I'll go talk to him now."

Her heart pounded in her ears and her palms started to sweat as she strolled back to the front door.

Mike saw her coming and turned to face her head on. His mouth shaped a smile and his eyes twinkled. "Hey, Joey. What's up?"

For her, life was an all or nothing type of thing. If she was going to do something, she didn't hold back. So she sucked in her stomach, stuck out her chest, and tossed her hair. "Nothing much. I was just standing over there watching you, and I couldn't help but wonder what you were doing after work tonight."

His smile widened. "Are you asking me out on a date?"

All or nothing. "I'm asking you to take me home with you."

A bark of laughter jumped from his lips and Joey's stomach dropped. "Never mind. Forget I said anything." She waved a hand and turned away. Before she went two steps, a large hand gripped her elbow and stopped her.

"Joey, wait!" He stepped in front of her, blocking her exit. "I'm sorry, I didn't mean to laugh. You just surprised me."

She held her head up. "It's okay, sugar. It was just a passing thought."

"Really? Because I don't like to be a passing thought, but I do like you." He crossed his arms over his massive chest and gazed at her steadily.

The next move was hers.

She cocked her hip and flashed him a flirty smile. "Then why don't we hook up after work and talk about this some more?"

He smiled and her heart skipped a beat. "I'd like that."

20

Samair was watching Joey work her wiles on the big doorman when she felt a solid presence behind her. Her nipples hardened and saliva pooled in her mouth. Val.

A hand touched her shoulder and his lips brushed against her ear when he spoke. "What's so interesting over there?"

She turned and faced him. "Joey's hitting on your bouncer."

"Hmm, they'd make an interesting couple. Beauty and the beast."

While Mike was no beast, she could see where the comparison came from. He pretty much dwarfed anyone who stood next him.

"Enough about them. You're early."

"I shared a cab with Joey. Figured I'd have a drink first and take a good look around so I can start imagining the show. I want to be able to use the stairs and everything, not just the stage." She looked at him. "Would that be okay?"

"Whatever you want," he murmured, his eyes liquid as his hands reached for the sash on her coat. "What are you hiding under here tonight?"

She let him undo the sash and hold the coat open. His eyes ran the length of her body, heating her insides to a melting point. Her insides clenched and her juices started to flow south. "Good enough?"

"Very, very bad," he muttered. "But in a very good way."

He pulled her coat closed. "Give me five minutes and we can go." He planted a fast and hard kiss on her lips and strode back into his office.

Arms wrapped around her from behind and a soft kiss was pressed to Samair's cheek. "Have fun tonight, okay? And stick close to Val. Don't wander off in the Dungeon without him."

Samair turned and smiled at Joey. "Yes, Mom. How'd it go with Mike?"

She blushed and her shoulders lifted in a delicate shrug. "We're going to talk more after work."

"Talk, huh?" Samair waggled her eyebrows.

Joey giggled like a little schoolgirl and they said good-bye.

Val came out of his office then, still dressed in dark dress slacks and button-down silk shirt, but his suit jacket was replaced with a leather one. Not his biker one from earlier that afternoon, but a different, stylized one that reeked of expensive taste. They were stopped three times by staff members on the way out the door and Samair wondered who managed the club when Val wasn't there.

"I don't have a second-in-command, but each area has a supervisor. Head bartender, head waitress, head of security. They all do their part and close up together if I'm not back." They exited through the back door of the club and stopped next to a gleaming black and chrome Harley. "Besides, I've got my cell phone if they need me."

He lifted one of the helmets from the seat of the bike and turned to Samair. "Ever been on one of these before?"

She looked at the helmet, the bike, her skirt, then finally into Val's face. "Can't we take a cab?"

"You'll love it. I promise."

He fitted the helmet onto her head while she practiced deep breathing and tried to calm her racing heart. Motorcycles were sexy when someone else was on them, but they scared the living shit out of her. There was no protection from an accident on those things; they were called death traps for a reason.

"Put your foot here and climb on," Val instructed.

"Don't you need to get on first?"

"I'm good. Let's get you settled first." He held her hand and patted the seat of the huge bike.

Adrenaline pumped through her system and she started to tremble. "I-I can't."

Val scrutinized her. "You trust me to keep you safe, right?"

"You, yes. But what about everyone else on the road?"

"Don't think about them. Just think about me." He stroked a finger down her cheek and toyed with her bottom lip. "Do you have panties on under that skirt?"

"A thong."

His eyes gleamed. "Take the skirt off."

"Huh?"

He slid his hand into her still-undone coat, kissed her softly, and traced his hand over her hip. "Your coat is long enough, and the skirt will just be uncomfortable on the bike anyway. Take it off. Now, before someone comes back here."

Arousal blended with the fear and adrenaline whipping through her.

With trembling fingers she undid the zipper at the back of her skirt and wiggled out of it.

Val held out his hand for the skirt. When she gave it to him, his features tightened and she recognized the hard edge of arousal he was trying to hide. She glanced down at herself and was shocked to see just how good she looked. The black boned corset cinched her waist and pushed her breasts up to an impossibly high level. If she sneezed, they'd pop out, and anyone looking at her knew it. The garter belt was a wide swath of stretch lace across her hips with the front and back extending lower on her thighs to reach the stockings. About two inches of pale, bare flesh peeked out from between the top of the stockings and the bottom edge of the lace, drawing attention to the satin triangle covering her pussy. She looked like a pin-up model.

"I'm going to fuck you while you wear that," Val growled before pulling her coat shut and cinching the belt at her waist. "Later."

Pleasure warmed her from the inside out and she didn't even notice the cool air drifting up under the coat. Okay, she noticed it, but she certainly didn't mind it.

Val tucked her skirt into a small storage bag on the side of the bike and turned to her. "Get on."

With her eyes locked on his steady gaze, she accepted his hand, stepped up and swung a leg over the bike. She gasped when her bare skin hit the cold seat and his grin turned evil.

He fussed with her coat for a moment. At first she thought he was making sure her ass was covered for the ride, but a slight breeze and a flutter of hot fingertips across her exposed butt cheeks told her he was doing just the op-posite. "Val! You're going to get us arrested if I flash the whole world."

"Not the whole world, babe." He slipped a leg over the bike and settled down in front of her. "Just whoever's directly behind us, and only if they're paying attention."

Val made quick work of putting his skullcap and helmet on before kick-starting the engine. The Harley roared to life, shaking and vibrating beneath her. "Oh!"

Val twisted around and grinned at her. "I told you you'd like it. Now hang on."

By the time he pulled the bike to a halt in front of a small brick building, Samair's fear was replaced by intense arousal and the thrill of some exhibitionism. Three cars had honked and flashed their lights in appreciation of her ass hanging out of her coat. The second car stayed with them for more than half of their drive.

When the giant vibrator between her legs finally shut off, she relaxed against Val's back for a minute, trying to catch her breath. He twisted around and offered her a hand to help her off before dismounting himself.

She'd readjusted her coat to make sure it covered every-thing and Val removed her helmet for her. When their eyes met again he was grinning like an idiot and she couldn't help but laugh.

"I can't believe I just did that."

He wrapped her in his arms and hugged her, then pressed a small kiss next to her ear, sending another shiver through her body before he spoke. "Ride on a Harley, or enjoy it so much?"

"Any of it!" She laughed and cuddled against him for a minute, reveling in the feel of his solid body and his arms around her. She wasn't trembling anymore, but she felt weak and shaky, poised on the edge. She pushed out of his arms and stepped back before she climbed up his body and wrapped her legs around his waist. Her sex throbbed and the patch of satin between her legs would be no barrier.

"Okay, give me my skirt and I'll slip it on real quick." She looked away from the couple that walked past them, not wanting to draw any attention to herself with eye contact.

"Uh-uh."

Her head snapped up. "Excuse me?"

Val shook his head, lips twitching. "You'll fit right in exactly as you are. You can even take the coat off once we're inside, if you want." He grabbed her hand and led her away from the bike.

"Val," she sputtered.

They turned a corner onto a busier street and Val kept walking. Samair ducked her head and tugged on his hand. When they reached the end of the building they came across a set of steps that led down, and Val gestured for her to lead the way. It was then that she realized not one person they'd passed had given her an odd look. In fact, nobody seemed to even notice her.

She wasn't sure she liked that.

No, she didn't like that at all. She wasn't a chicken shit, and she wasn't a wallflower. She was a sexy, kick-ass lingerie designer with a super-sexy lover by her side. Energy stirred deep inside and a calm confidence settled over her. She could do this. She could do anything if she set her mind to it.

21

Samair reached the bottom step and stood in front of the linebacker in a business suit who was stationed there. She met his eyes and flashed a naughty smile as his appreciative gaze ran over her from head to toe before he looked over her shoulder at Val.

"Guests of Karl Dawson," Val said from behind her. His voice was strong, his hand at her back solid.

The doorman checked his clipboard before holding the door open. "Welcome to the Dungeon, sir."

Samair passed him and started down another set of stairs. These were a bit steeper, and difficult to descend in her heels, so she went slowly. The music got louder with each step and by the time she reached the bottom—and another linebacker—she was feeling sultry, seductive, and ready for anything.

"Master Dawson is along the back wall, sir. Second booth to the left of the bar," said the linebacker as soon as Val stood next to her.

Val thanked him for his directions and steered her deeper into the cavernous room. Blue lights, low ceilings, and chains along the walls made it resemble a real dungeon. It was only a Wednesday night, but the place was packed.

Packed with people dressed in leather, latex, and silk. Some wore masks that brought Mardi Gras to mind, others wore even less than her corset and coat. Val steered her through the crowd silently, letting her drink in her fill.

Everything looked so . . . erotic. Always a tactile person, Samair had to fist her hands at her sides to keep from reaching out to touch everything and everyone they passed. She wanted to get a closer look at the latex bodysuit. Or the contraption made of leather straps crisscrossed over one shirtless guy's chest and back that blended into a leash held by the woman seated next to him.

Glad for Val's guiding hand, she followed him blindly while her head swiveled constantly, taking in the whole experience.

When Val stopped in front of a circular booth occupied by a couple, it didn't faze her that the aroused expression on the woman's face ensured there was some obvious fondling going on under the table. Instead the first thing Samair noticed was that the white dress she was wearing was completely see-through and her nipples were painted or tattooed or something.

Then she noticed that both of the guy's hands were on the tabletop and the woman was playing with herself, in full view of him. Putting on a show *for* him.

Val grinned and shook his head before speaking loudly. "Karl, this is Samair. Samair, my good friend Karl."

Samair gazed at the man lounging in front of her. His blond curls and brown eyes did not make him look soft or innocent, despite the fact that he was dressed simply in a black T-shirt with no leather or studs in sight.

"Samair." He held out his hand and she shook it as the exotic beauty he'd been watching edged her way out of the booth and walked away without a word.

Val urged her into the booth and slid in after her while she tried to ignore Karl's sharp gaze. The men talked quietly until the waitress arrived and took their drink order. When Samair couldn't stand it anymore, she turned to the man next to her and looked him over.

He was beautiful.

Sharp cheekbones, straight nose, full lips. There was a small scar through his left eyebrow that only made him look better, and the edges of a tattoo that crept out from under his collar added to his bad-boy appeal.

He turned his head and met her gaze head on. "So, you're Val's new plaything, huh? I can see why he likes you."

The insulting flick of his gaze to her cleavage made it clear he thought she was nothing but a big set of tits.

"Karl," Val growled.

"No, it's okay, Val." Samair smiled and put her hand on his thigh under the table. "If Karl has a problem with women, there's nothing I can do about it. If he has a problem with me, he needs to spit it out."

Val didn't bother to hide his smirk at Karl's surprise. Samair was nobody's fool.

He watched, body tense, as his friend and his lover locked gazes. Then, Karl leaned forward and kissed Samair on the cheek. "No problem with you, my dear."

Samair's hand tightened on Val's thigh, and relief flowed through him. Karl's opinion of women had never been real great, they were always just too easy for him. Being a divorce lawyer probably didn't help him see the best in women, or in relationships, either. But lately Karl's attitude toward women had really soured, and Val was glad to see that he was still able to recognize a good one when she was right in front of him. And Samair was a good one.

She flashed a bright smile at Karl and settled back in her seat. "Good. Then since this is your scene, can I pick your brain?"

He opened his hands, palms up. "Anything I can do to help make this fetish and fantasy show a success, I'm all for. Pick away."

The waitress brought Val's beer, and he noticed Samair had only ordered a bottled water. He took a minute while the waitress flirted with Karl to check on Samair. "You doing okay?"

She turned her head and their lips almost touched. Her eyes went soft and she pressed a light kiss to his mouth. "I'm fine," she said, and rubbed her hand on his thigh.

"You don't want something stronger to drink?" Christ, if she kept touching him like that he was going to be more than fine damn fast.

As if she read his mind, her hand crept up his thigh and her smiled turned devilish. "I don't need alcohol to feel good when I'm with you. Especially after riding that monstrous vibrator."

"I'd like to use a real vibrator on you." The thought of having her laid out before him, open to whatever he wanted to do to bring her pleasure made his dick hard.

"Would you two like me to get a private room?" Karl's light voice held an edge of dark interest as it cut through the sexual haze that had been descending.

It was his turn to leave it to Samair to answer. Was she interested in playing while they were there?

Her cheeks flushed and her fingers tightened on his thigh,

but she shook her head. "A threesome with two men *is* on my list of fantasies—"

Val's gaze sharpened. "Two men, hmm?"

"Oh, yeah." She nodded. "I think I'd enjoy being the center of attention, being touched and teased and overwhelmed with the sensation of two men wanting me." Heat swamped Samair's insides and she squeezed her thighs together. "But first . . . the reason we're here."

She turned to Karl. "Where do people buy this stuff? I mean, I've been in a lot of lingerie stores and a few of the local sex shops, but I've never seen anything like . . . well, like that." She nodded at a woman who was approaching their table, her eyes locked on Karl like a target. She had long blond hair that fell in curls down her back and was wearing a few shiny pieces of black PVC held over her breasts, crotch, and ass by crisscrossing laces.

She had a nice body but the outfit was too over-the-top for Val's taste. Karl must've agreed, because when he saw her coming he met her gaze, gave one shake of his head, and she stopped dead in her tracks. Val could see the indecision on her face: should she push her luck, or leave him be? She must've had some sense of self-preservation because her lips tightened and she turned away.

"Wow." Samair chuckled. "What are you, a God or something?"

Val held back a chuckle of his own; he was completely

content to sit back, nurse his beer, and watch the two of them get to know each other. He wondered how Karl would explain his magic with women to a woman.

With a twist and a quick wiggle Samair shucked her coat and sat between the two men in her corset, garter, and stockings. She didn't push for an answer from Karl when he just shrugged and grinned. Instead she started to point out outfits, ask questions, and listen to Karl's explanations. The whole time she kept her hand on Val's thigh, stroking her thumb back and forth.

At one point Karl waved another girl over and had her turn around so Samair could check out something on the dress. She leaned across Val's lap to reach the girl's dress and nuzzled her breasts against his semi-hard cock. When she gave an extra wiggle and pressed into him on purpose, he sharply smacked her exposed ass and they all laughed.

She was truly amazing. A lady, a seductress, a vixen, and completely open. With her there was no wondering what she was thinking or head games. He loved it, and he could see that Karl responded well to it, too.

Val eyed Samair as she gestured over her body, trying to get them to visualize some outfit. She'd said being with two men was one of her fantasies, and he'd promised to fulfill those fantasies. He glanced at Karl thoughtfully.

The lights dimmed even more and the music lowered. "Time for the second show," Karl announced.

Samair looked blank. "Show?"

"Wednesday nights is show night here at the Dungeon. Dominants put on demonstrations of their skills."

Karl explained that the skills included everything from spanking to bondage to knife or wax play.

"Knife play?" She turned to Val. "Just so you know, knives will never play a part in *any* of my fantasies."

He laughed and shook his head. "No arguments here."

They turned their attention to the stage. A well-built guy wearing only a pair of tight black shorts was getting strapped onto an X cross. The statuesque woman at his side picked up a microphone.

"For some people there is a very thin line between pleasure and pain. It takes open communication, trust, and a deft touch to make sure that your submissive gets what he or she needs from you. Tonight I'd like to show you how you can use your basic household clothespins to get an idea of your sub's sensitivity." She stepped back and put the microphone down. Sexy saxophone music swelled gently and she began to work on her man.

Instead of watching the show, Val watched Samair's reaction to it. She'd tensed up, her thumb had stopped stroking him, and she was leaning forward intently.

"Oh my God." The color drained from her cheeks and she slumped back against the booth.

He met Karl's curious gaze before speaking. "What's wrong, Samair?"

"I know him. The guy on the cross, I know him." She looked stunned. "I can't believe it."

"You'd be amazed at how many people are into different types of kinks," Karl said softly. "Like everything else in the world, it takes all types."

"Samair?" Concern swelled inside Val. She looked more than stunned. She looked . . . hurt. "Who is it?"

She turned her head and met his gaze. "My brother."

22

Samair didn't sleep much that night. Shortly into the clothes-pin demonstration it had become obvious that Brett was getting a hard-on in his shorts, and that had just been too much information for her to handle. She'd only had to look at Val and he'd read her mind.

"Let's get out of here," he'd said, and slid out of the booth.

Surprisingly, Karl had thrown some cash on the table and left with them. All three were silent during the short walk to Val's bike. When they got there, Samair noticed another big Harley parked next to it, this one red and chrome. Karl had beaten them to the bar, and she hadn't even noticed the other Harley when they'd parked.

Mind you, Val had kept her pretty distracted by not giving her skirt back. Thank God her brother hadn't seen her in there. She didn't think she could've dealt with that.

While Val helped her onto the bike and fitted the helmet on her head, Karl pulled his from a small side storage pouch like the one Val had on his bike, before turning back to say good-bye. "It was nice meeting you, Samair. Take it easy."

The men nodded to each other and climbed onto their bikes. Despite the fact that her mind was millions of miles away, trying to bury the sight of her younger brother strapped to a bondage cross, she'd noticed that Val and Karl had an ease between them that spoke of years in a close relationship. Almost like brothers.

The ride back to her place hadn't been nearly as thrilling as the ride to the club, and when they got to the apartment, he'd walked her to her door, plastered her against it with his body, and kissed her until she was incoherent.

Then he'd walked away.

"What?" she'd sputtered at his back.

"I think you've had enough excitement for one night, babe," he said from the stairwell five feet away. "I'll talk to you tomorrow."

At first she'd been stunned, but once she was inside she realized he was smarter than her. She'd have happily buried all thoughts in mindless sex, but he'd known that wasn't what she'd really needed. And *that* only added to her confusion.

She wasn't sure she wanted him to know her that well.

Sleep had been elusive. After tossing and turning for an hour, she was up and pacing the small apartment, mentally ranting about people pretending to be someone they're not.

Lisa, Kevin, Rosa, Brett. Shit, even *she'd* been pretending for a while.

No, she hadn't been pretending—she'd been denying. There was a difference.

Lisa and Kevin had deceived her, intentionally. Rosa had deliberately claimed Samair's work as her own, which was why she'd quit. They'd been pretending. They were liars.

What category did Brett fall into?

He was the youngest in the family. The only boy and the one who *should've* been the wild child. But no . . . he'd been a good student and an even better athlete. They'd been close when they were growing up; Brett hadn't cared that Samair was always in trouble.

"With you always in detention and mouthing off to the parentals, they don't pay attention to my being half an hour late for curfew," he'd once said with a laugh.

Hockey scholarships had paid for his education and he was already making a great name for himself in the junior leagues. He was expected to go pro as soon as he graduated from university the next year.

And he was apparently into a bit of pain.

When four o'clock came and went Samair realized that

Joey wasn't going to make it home, and that she wasn't going to be able to concentrate on the design ideas she'd come up with at the Dungeon until she talked to Brett. She took a couple of aspirin and crawled back into the empty bed and lay there, hugging the pillow and cursing herself for letting Val walk away.

23

The sound of Joey's off-key singing woke Samair up a mere three hours later. She rolled over with a groan and buried her face into the pillow. Then she lifted it and sniffed the air.

"Bacon?" she called out hopefully.

"And pancakes," Joey called back.

She dragged her ass out of bed and stumbled to the breakfast bar. Joey, angel that she was, already had a glass of ice cold Diet Coke waiting for her.

Samair sipped her cold caffeine and watched Joey flip a pancake. A minute later she turned from the stove with a huge stupid-ass grin and set a plate full of food in front of Samair. "We didn't have sex."

Samair bit into a piece of bacon and waited.

"I went home with Mike after work last night, and he made us coffee and we talked all night. Well, not all night, since we didn't get done at the bar until after three, and he had to get ready for work at seven. He has a day job, and he lives with his brother, but his brother is out of town right now so we had the place to ourselves. You know I don't normally drink coffee, I prefer tea, and I never drink coffee at three in the morning, but Sammie, he told me straight up that he wasn't interested in just fucking me. He said he wanted more. More than one night. More than just a lay. It was incredible." She gave a dreamy sigh, then straightened up and looked Samair in the eye. "Now don't think I've totally lost it. I mean, he's just a guy. And guys play games. But he was so sweet and sexy at the same time."

Samair watched her friend in amazement. Energetic, sassy, and slightly raunchy Joey Kent had a new soft edge to her. Like a schoolgirl in love. It looked good on her, too. "Sweet *and* sexy. It's a good combination."

She grabbed another piece of bacon to munch on.

Joey quieted down and fiddled with her fork, not meeting Samair's eyes. "Do you think maybe he's scamming me?"

Samair's heart clenched. She looked so happy . . . and so scared. Kevin had been a "nice guy," and look what had happened with him. Her brother was a "nice guy" who got off on pain-pleasure stimuli. Yet she looked at Joey, so hopeful, and she couldn't bring herself to vent to her all her thoughts about fake people.

Besides, she'd never exchanged more than two words with the bouncer. Who was she to judge? "What do your instincts say?"

"I don't know," Joey shrugged. "I think he's for real. I really do. But what guy says no to sex so that he can have more than one night? I mean, that's the way girls think, not guys."

"That's a true but very narrow point of view." She frowned at Joey. "Aren't you the same person who always encouraged me to stop doing what was expected and do what I wanted to do?"

"Yeah."

"It seems to me that maybe Mike *is* doing what he wants, going after what he wants—that would be you—instead of doing what people think he should do—which would be jumping at the easy sex."

Joey's mouth gaped, then she snapped her jaw shut and color flooded her cheeks. "You're right."

"I know." Samair grinned and dug into her pancakes.

Their eyes met and they both laughed. "So how was the Dungeon?"

Samair thought about it for a minute. "Educational."

Joey snorted.

"Educational? Okay, I get that you might've seen some

things, maybe even done some things . . ." She raised her eyebrows at that. "But that's a weird way to describe a night at a sex club with a stud like Valentine Ward."

Samair needed to tread carefully. She didn't want to talk about Brett and open that whole can of worms until she'd had a chance to talk *to* him.

"I went there to look at the outfits, remember?"

"Yes. And I remember who you were going there with." Joey stuffed a forkful of pancake in her mouth and stared at her expectantly.

"Have you ever been on a Harley?"

"Oh yeah. Baby those give good vibrations, don't they?"

And just like that, the conversation moved on.

Brett was already at their favorite sushi restaurant when Samair arrived. She'd called him right after Joey had floated out of the apartment on her way to work, and asked him to meet her for an early lunch.

She was five minutes late, and he was already seated at a table near the window. She tapped on it, and waved on her way past, laughing when he jumped.

Ignoring the stares, Samair swept past the hostess and plopped down in the chair across from him with a tight smile. She still hadn't figured out how to broach the subject foremost on her mind.

"So, little brother, how's life?"

Brett grinned, his blue eyes bright. "Pretty good, pretty good. You're looking pretty cheerful for an unemployed and homeless bum."

She grimaced. "Is that what Cherish is calling me, or Mom?"

He laughed. "C'mon, they wouldn't say something like that. You know they prefer to speak in euphemisms. 'Samair is just planning her career right now.' 'She's between boyfriends at the moment.' "

"Actually I have some big news on the career front, but I don't really want you to share it with the family. I think you can keep a secret?"

"Hey, I never told Cherish that it was you who plastered that photo of her and Chris Salter all over the school locker rooms."

"True, and I appreciate that."

The waitress arrived and took their order, practically ignoring Samair and flirting with Brett shamelessly. When she walked away, Samair watched Brett check out the girl's swinging hips and bit her tongue.

"So, what's the news?" He lifted his coffee mug and grinned at her. "You submit an application to be on *Project Runway* and get accepted?"

Samair laughed. "God no!"

Brett could always make her laugh. Somehow, he always

managed to cut through the bullshit and make her smile. If it hadn't been for him, she'd have run away from home by the time she was fifteen.

"Better. I got asked to host a fashion show, featuring my own line of lingerie, at a private party at Club Risqué."

His eyes widened. "That's huge, sis!"

Brett lifted his mug to her and she clinked it with her glass. He really was a great brother. Always there for her.

He stared at her a moment, eyebrows slowly drawing down into a frown.

"What?"

"Why don't you want the family to know? This would be the perfect thing to get them to lay off and let you go for it."

"The theme for the show is Fetish and Fantasy. Not exactly the type of show I think Mom and Dad would enjoy."

"No shit."

She stirred the ice in her glass with the straw, watching him from under her lashes. "Do you think they'd freak?"

"I think they wouldn't understand." He sat back to let the waitress refill his coffee, but he didn't even look at her, so she walked away when she was done. "Mom and Dad, and even Cherish, they're not bad people . . ."

"I know that." She did. She knew her family loved her; they just didn't understand anything, or anyone who didn't want the same things they wanted.

Ding, ding, ding.

Brett knew what she knew. That their family wasn't as perfect as everyone liked to believe, and that some things, some dreams, some *desires*, were better kept to oneself.

He wasn't lying about who he was or pretending to be someone he wasn't. He was just keeping his own business to himself. She could understand that. She didn't want to tell the whole world she was working her way through an imaginary list of fantasies with an older man she barely knew.

A weight lifted from her shoulders and she relaxed back in her seat. Brett was barely twenty-six years old. Old enough to make his own choices and be his own person. She could respect that.

"Are they still harping on your hockey?" she asked with a wry smile.

"Yeah. Dad keeps trying to set me up on interviews. The I'm-not-done-with-school-yet argument is only going to work for another few months."

"Then?"

He laughed. "I'm hoping by then you'll be making enough of a splash with this business of yours that they won't freak when I tell them I'm sticking with hockey."

She shook her head at him. "I love you, little brother."

24

After lunch with Brett, Samair took her sketchbook and settled on the loveseat with a bag of microwave popcorn and a huge glass of soda. She wasn't hungry, but the muse was, and Samair needed inspirational designs fast.

Sure enough, the combination of salt, sugar, and caffeine worked . . . and four hours later she had over a dozen rough sketches. Images of things she'd seen the night before, things she'd found on the Internet, things she liked, all blended into some of the wildest things she'd ever created, and some of the softest, too.

The best thing about all of the designs was she really only needed three basic patterns that she could build on. She had one corset design that she could easily alter to make different looks and accessorize to suit either a dominant or submissive look.

Thank God Tara was a bit of an exhibitionist; she was going to need a model willing to be almost naked for a couple of the outfits. Her imagination had really gotten into the erotic spirit of things with a cupless bondage bra and a net bodysuit.

Joey wasn't exactly shy with her body either, so that gave her two models. Kelly was iffy, but that was okay because not every outfit required massive exposure. She needed to ask Joey if she'd found a few others willing to model for her. They'd have to meet next week to make sure everything fit, and go over the floor plan.

The floor plan. She needed to utilize the whole place to make sure that everyone there got a look at the products.

She got up and cleaned the breakfast dishes, keeping her hands busy so her mind could roam free. She pictured the club, and where and how she'd want the models to walk—or to dance?

Her cell phone rang and she wiped her hands dry on her jeans before flipping it open.

"Hey, babe. How are you today?" Val. The warmth in his voice brought a soft smile to her face.

"Doing good. Really good actually."

"Glad to hear it."

"Thanks for last night," she said quietly. She picked up

her pencil and started doodling on the blank page in front of her. She was a little unsure how to say what she'd been thinking. "About last night. At first I didn't get why you weren't sticking around . . . you know, to umm, to fuck me in the corset like you'd promised. But after you left, I got it."

"You had other things on your mind last night. I'm a selfish man; I want you to be fully aware, and into anything that happens between us." He laughed softly. "Besides, I expect you to wear that corset for me again sometime."

Heat rushed to her sex. She swallowed and tried to speak naturally. "I had lunch with Brett today. My brother."

"How did it go?"

"It was good. He's still the same guy I grew up with. When I went there I'd planned to confront him, but I realized that it didn't matter. He's allowed to have a private life, too, and it's none of my business. It's not like I want him knowing—" She cut herself off.

"Knowing what?" His soft chuckle echoed over the phone line. "That you have an adventurous streak yourself?"

She relaxed. "Exactly."

Talking to him was nice. He understood.

She looked at her doodling and realized she'd been drawing little hearts and filling them in. Shit.

Taking a deep breath, she tried to get her head back in the real world. "Are you at Risqué?"

"Heading in right now."

"Think I could drop in and walk around while it's still closed? To get a good mental idea of how I want to lay things out for the show." Mental images of the club just weren't doing it. Plus, getting him alone in his office sounded like a real good idea right about then. She could thank him properly for his care and concern.

"Sure, just use the doorbell at the back. Kelsey will be stocking the bar and she'll let you in."

They said their good-byes and she snapped the phone shut.

With anticipation fluttering in her stomach, she started for the closet. She knew just what she wanted to wear for this little visit.

The Hog rumbled beneath him and the wind whipped through his hair as Val made his way to the club. Soon the weather would turn and he'd have to put the bike away for the winter. He had an old Camaro stashed in Karl's garage that was his winter car, but he'd keep driving the bike as long as he could.

Hopefully, he'd be able to make one last road trip before it was time to park it. Karl would certainly be up for it. He wondered what it would take to get Samair to go with them. Her attitude in dealing with Karl had been top notch. Val chuckled to himself. Women were too easy for Karl and he needed one to stand up to him and put him in his place every now and then.

The night before certainly hadn't turned out the way he'd thought it would. He was still hard-pressed to pick a part of the night that was his favorite. Especially now that he'd talked to Samair and found out she was doing okay. If she'd been hurt by his taking her there, he'd have felt like shit.

The ride to the Dungeon, with Samair's legs hugging him and her body pressing against his, had been great. It had felt almost . . . right. Like she belonged there, on the bike with him.

He'd never been able to coax Vera onto the Harley; she'd been way too concerned about who would see her to care how it would feel, or how it would make him feel.

The wonderment on Samair's face when she'd climbed off the bike had told him that he probably wouldn't have to beg to get her on it again. The expression had remained as they walked through the underground club, and it made him want to show her the world. It wasn't like she was innocent—a woman that played his body the way she did was no vir-gin—but she was ingenuous. Her pleasure and enthusiasm were pure and honest.

She didn't play head games, and he liked that.

When Val pulled up at the back door to Risqué he was feeling damn good. He entered the club through the back door and started down the small corridor. The door to the walk-in cooler was open so he stopped in the doorway to talk to his head bartender. "Everything go all right last night, Kelsey?"

"Smooth as a baby's butt, boss." The petite brunette hefted a case of Bud onto the trolley she had set up, then planted her hands on her hips. "How was your night?"

Val smiled. Kelsey had worked for him since he'd opened the place. They weren't friends, but she was a sweetheart, and she was valuable to him. "Not as smooth as yours, but still good. I like the new color, it suits you better than the purple."

"Yeah?" She fingered a lock of hair. "I wasn't so sure. It was between orange or blue, and I've done blue before . . . so orange it is."

"It's perfect. Halloween is coming soon, so you'll be considered enthusiastic."

"Shit! I didn't even think of Halloween. Oh no, the orange has to go. Maybe green," she muttered as she hefted another case of beer.

He'd knew that would get her.

Val used to offer to help her with the beer, or bring one of the guys in early for the lifting, but Kelsey was nothing if not stubborn, and he'd learned to let her do it her way.

"Hey, boss," she called out as he turned away.

"Yeah?"

"Your ex is at the bar, and she's pissy because I wouldn't let her into your office to wait for you."

Great. "Thanks."

Dread settled on his shoulders. It was never good news when Vera came by the club. He shoved the swinging door open and strode inside. "What do you want, Vera?"

"Is that any way to greet a friend?" She smiled from her perch by the main bar.

His steps didn't falter as he crossed the floor to the stairs. "You're not a friend."

"Tsk, tsk, Val. I was much more than a friend at one point."

Val didn't respond. He wasn't going to get into a discussion about the past with her.

She followed him up the stairs and into his office. Ignoring her, he took off his jacket and hung it on the rack, then sat behind his desk and booted up the computer.

"You're looking good, Valentine." Vera seated herself on the sofa, crossing her legs and smiling at him seductively.

"Thank you. I'm feeling good." Or he had been until he saw her.

"Feeling better than when we were together?"

His gaze snapped to her. "Why do you care?"

"You live in a crappy apartment, you sold your Camaro, and you're struggling to make your bank payments. I want to make sure you're okay."

His impatience reared and he put down the pencil he'd picked up before he snapped it in two. His tolerance for

Vera's games had ended the night he'd left her, but he really didn't want her to know how easily she could get under his skin. "I don't have time for this. What do you want, Vera?"

She stood up and prowled toward him. She came close and perched on the corner of his desk. This time, when she crossed her legs, her foot brushed against his leg in a deliberate caress. "I want to invest in Risqué."

He pushed his chair back and stood, crossing his arms over his chest. "I'm not looking for investors."

"Oh? Have you paid off the bank loan then?"

"You know I haven't."

"Then why not let me invest? I can certainly afford it."

"You've never had an interest in the club. No reason for you to start now."

"Oh, but there is a reason." She leaned forward, resting her hand on his arm. "I want to fix things between us, to make it all up to you."

"Let it go, Vera. You don't want to make it up to me. You hate that I was the one to call our marriage off. It pisses you off that a lowly club owner—a *thug*, I believe you called me—would have the nerve to walk away from you." He gave a derisive snort. "You want to control me, and it's not going to happen."

She slid off his desk and smiled viciously. "You're going to lose this club, and then you're going to regret being so stubborn with me. It's a woman's prerogative to change her mind, and I might not want you or the club anymore."

Val bit his tongue to keep from reminding her that he knew from experience just how fickle she was. Instead, he watched her slim hips swing from side to side as she walked out of his office.

He sat down, pulled out a legal pad, and grabbed his pencil. He couldn't let Vera get to him. Samair was coming down to talk about the fashion show and he had several ideas to run by her.

Pencil poised over paper, and all he could see was Vera's vicious smile. He leaned back against his chair, closed his eyes, and counted to ten.

And when he opened his eyes, he straightened up and glanced through the wall of windows . . . and saw Vera talking to Samair.

25

Samair recognized the brunette heading toward her right away. They locked stares when Samair hit the top of the steps on her way to Val's office, and Samair was shocked when the woman smiled at her.

Then again, it wasn't exactly a friendly smile.

"I don't think Valentine wants any visitors right now. He's in a bit of a mood," she said when they were only a couple of feet apart.

Both women stopped, and Samair gave a small smile. "Really? He was in a great mood when I spoke to him a short time ago."

"I have that effect on him." The woman laughed and held

out her hand. "I'm Vera Duggin, Valentine's ex-wife. I don't think I've met you before."

"Samair Jones. Val's friend." Oh, how tempting it was to say *lover*, but—oh, hell. "And lover."

Vera's smile softened, her tongue darted out to smooth across her lips and her hand held Samair's for a moment longer. "I'm not surprised. You're a very beautiful woman."

A tingle of awareness ran through Samair. "Thank you."

"Not many women embrace their curves anymore, and it's a shame. A lush figure like yours just brings all sorts of possibilities to mind."

A telling silence fell as they gazed at each other. Vera's gaze darkened and she shifted closer.

"I thought you were done here, Vera."

Samair started at Val's voice. For a minute there she'd been completely absorbed by the tension between herself and Vera.

He stepped around Vera and put a hand on Samair's back. As if he thought she needed protection.

"We were just chatting, Valentine." Vera smirked and stepped back. "I'm surprised you allow your lovers to visit you here. You have changed."

Val's lips tightened and his body stiffened. Samair leaned into his side comfortingly as she spoke. "I'm here on business, actually. Risqué is hosting a fashion show for my new design label and there are some things we needed to go over."

"You're a fashion designer?"

"Yes, mostly lingerie and costumes. You seem like a woman who loves sexy lingerie. You should be sure to come to the show . . . spend some money." She flashed her a cheeky grin.

Vera chuckled and slid a glance at Val. "I do love sexy things. Thank you for the invitation. I'll make it a point to attend. For now, I'll leave you two to your work." She stepped around them. "Bye for now, lovers."

Neither of them moved until Vera was out of earshot, then Samair turned to Val. He was stiff and still, with the same completely blank yet somehow furious expression that he'd had the last time she'd seen Vera walking away from him.

Her chest tightened. He'd been married. And he was still in contact with his ex. There was so much about him that she didn't know, but there was one thing she did know: she didn't want to see him like that.

So, she stood on tiptoe, braced her hands on Val's stiff shoulders, and pressed her lips to his. When she pulled back, the frost had eased from his features. Decision made, she took his hand in hers, turned, and led the way into his office where she pushed him gently onto the leather sofa.

Neither of them spoke. She didn't want to talk. She didn't want to know what had happened to his marriage, or what his ex-wife was doing there. All she wanted was to make his tension disappear, and make them both feel very, very good.

Her fingers lifted and she started to unbutton her blouse. "I wanted to show you one of my designs. It's a few years old, but I think you'll like it just the same."

His eyes turned to molten chocolate as he held her stare. He didn't watch her fingers or look at the slowly appearing nakedness; his focus was on her.

And it revved her engine into high gear in no time flat.

Her blouse dropped to the floor with her skirt only a split second behind it. Feet shoulder width apart, she stood proud, dressed in a pink satin push-up bra that barely held her breasts, and a matching garter belt and stockings that framed the blond nest of her curls like a picture.

She licked her lips and boldly met his gaze. "Do you like?"

He stood and prowled toward her. When he was inches away, his breath whispering across her lips, he cupped her head in both hands and slammed his mouth down on hers.

It was as if all they couldn't say to each other was put into that kiss. Mouths opened and his tongue delved and dominated while his hands held her still and she surrendered.

Every bone in her body melted under the heat of passion as he took what she offered freely. He stepped forward, walking her backward until she hit the wall and the full length of his body pressed against her. Pinning her there and holding her upright under his onslaught.

Samair clutched at his shoulders and whimpered. He released her mouth and dragged his lips across her jaw and down her neck while his hands slid over her shoulders, down her arms, to her waist. One hand skimmed up her rib cage to cup a breast for his traveling lips while the other continued down, over her belly, until he was dipping between her thighs.

A moan slid from her throat as she arched into his hands. Hot blood pounded through her veins on its way to her sex. Val tugged the edge of her bra and sucked a rigid nipple into his mouth at the same time a long finger traced the length of her slit. "Please," she begged.

The finger skimmed across her wetness again and he lifted his head. He looked down into her eyes. "Please what?"

She opened her mouth but no words came out. Her chest rose and fell as she panted and her hips pressed forward, wordlessly telling him what she wanted. What she needed.

His fingers tickled over her pussy, lightly brushing her clit and disappearing. "Tell me," he demanded. "Tell me what you want."

"Touch me." She pushed the words out between gasps for more oxygen.

As soon as the words left her lips, his hand cupped her core and a finger entered her body. He rocked his hand, the palm rubbing against her clit while another finger joined the first and she whimpered again. Using his teeth, he tugged the edge of her bra over her other breast and sucked that nipple into his mouth.

There was no gentleness as he suckled at her. His teeth worried the rigid tip and his hand rocked against her with strength and purpose. Suddenly, pleasure ripped through her and she cried out, clutching at Val and bucking against him as her insides clenched and she came.

Before she could recover, Val unzipped his pants, wedged his hips between her legs, grabbed her hands and pinned them to the wall above her head. He buried his head in the crook of her neck and entered her with one swift thrust.

Chest to chest, belly to belly, he held both her wrists in one hand and hooked her leg over his hip with the other. They both groaned at the deeper penetration.

He cupped her ass and Samair lifted her other leg and hooked her heels together behind his back. "Yes," he grunted. His hips pumped and his cock shafted in and out, hitting her deep, and chasing passionate sounds from her with every stroke.

Pressure built rapidly and she tightened her inner muscles, wrenching a groan from Val. His hand tightened on her ass, holding her still as he picked up speed and fucked her harder. He bent his knees and angled deeper, hitting her pleasure spot and making her cry out. Her body tensed and she went over the edge into another orgasm, pleasure extending from her sex to every nerve center in her body. Her orgasm set off Val's and he bit her neck as a guttural cry escaped from him.

Minutes later he released her wrists and her arms went

around him. She rubbed his back and shoulders with one hand while the other stroked his hair, keeping his head at her shoulder as they both caught their breath.

Slowly, his hand left her ass and he lowered her so her feet touched the floor. He eased away and straightened her bra, carefully tucking her breasts back in before bending to kiss each satin-covered tip.

Samair raised a hand and cupped his cheek. He met her gaze and they both smiled.

"I like the lingerie," he said with a straight face.

She laughed softly and nodded. Things were good.

26

In general, Samair wouldn't want to live anywhere but Vancouver, but there were certainly days when it sucked. Days when it felt like the rain would never let up.

Whatever Val's reason for letting her do a show at Risqué, Samair wasn't going to question it again. It didn't really matter what the reason was. What mattered was this was her chance to launch Trouble in a way that could really make a difference.

The night before she'd spent some time on the computer looking at fetish websites, as well as lingerie ones. Her designs were unique, but not out of this world, and to make them work for what had become the Fetish and Fantasy show, the right material for each piece was essential.

So far, leather, PVC, and various types of lace were on her list, but not everything was making it into her basket. Prices were high and she wasn't sure she was going to be able to get everything she needed.

Panic was starting to get a grip when her phone rang. She snatched it out of her pocket before the second peal could sound. While she enjoyed the convenience of cell phones, and knew it was a smart thing to have one, she hated the sound of them ringing in public.

"Hello," she said without checking the caller ID.

"Samair," a voice singsonged. "I've been looking for you."

Remembering that she now gave out business cards with her cell phone number, she refrained from snapping. Instead, she rolled her eyes and focused on the bolt of netting in front of her. "How can I help you?"

"Well, for starters you can tell me why my favorite salesgirl isn't at Rosa's anymore, or why her house phone has been disconnected, and why I had to read on a flyer that my girl is having a fashion show!"

"Ginger?" A grin split Samair's face. "Oh my God, it's great to hear your voice! How are you?"

"I'm fantastic as always. And it seems like you are, too. Fetish and Fantasy show, hmmm. You are *full* of surprises."

Samair quickly walked out the front door of the fabric warehouse to stand outside and talk. The rain had turned to a light drizzle so she stayed under the door awning.

Ginger had been her coworker at Rosa's for years. When Samair was working part-time in college, Ginger was the full-time girl. She'd quit just before Bethany got pregnant and left, and while she'd drop by and say hi to Samair every now and then, Samair had never really thought of her as a close friend.

But there was no denying the sound of Ginger's voice hit a certain button for her. "Things change. Rosa's place sucked without you and Bethany, and the opportunity for the show came at just the right time, so I went for it. Or I should say I'm trying to go for it."

"What do you mean *trying*? If I remember correctly that word isn't part of your vocabulary."

"Well, starting up this design label was a bit of a spur of the moment thing, and while I do have a savings, it's nowhere near as much as it should be."

"Ohhh. Money issues huh, doll?"

There was a rustling sound and Ginger's voice faded behind running water. "Ginger?"

"I'm here, sorry. Had to rinse this film or I'd lose it."

Samair felt like an idiot. Here she'd been going on about herself and she'd never even thought to ask how Ginger's new business was going. It seemed like everyone wanted to work for themselves these days. "How's the photography going?"

"Doing good. Life is good."

"Still with Jason, eh?" Samair laughed.

"Yeah, the man o' my dreams. Listen, hun, I have to run right now but I had to track you down and tell you Bethany and I are coming to your show. We wouldn't miss it for the world. If you need anything, anything at all, you call, okay?"

Emotion clogged Samair's throat. "I will."

"And Samair . . ."

"Yes?"

"One thing I learned when starting up my business was that if you have a decent limit on your credit card, which I know you do, a lot of places will let you set up a business account to pay monthly, *and* you can barter for discounts."

"Thank you."

Samair hung up the phone and had to stand outside for a few extra minutes. When she'd walked in on Kevin and Lisa, she'd thought she had no friends left other than Joey, who she'd slowly turned away from over the years. But the phone call from Ginger was proof that she had been wrong.

Sometimes being wrong was a beautiful thing.

27

"Roll over," Samair commanded.

A dark eyebrow winged upward. "You said on my back."

"And now I've changed my mind." She climbed off the bed. "You'd better be on your front when I return."

Samair went straight for the front room where she'd left her backpack when she'd arrived earlier that night. Or morning. Whatever. She'd been working day and night on her designs and when she'd glanced at the clock to see it was almost two in the morning and she was still wide awake, she'd made her first booty call ever.

Val had picked her up after closing the club, and taken her home with him. As soon as they'd walked in the door,

Val had taken complete control, stripped her naked, and bent her over for a good hard fuck that had left them both breathless.

Now it was her turn.

Shaking her head, she picked up the bag she was always leaving in his hallway and headed back to the bedroom. She'd come prepared to make her fantasy a reality, but she'd been so distracted by Val himself that she'd forgotten her plan.

Focused on what she'd wanted all along, when she got back to the bedroom she was happy to see Val had rolled over and folded his arms under his chin. She dropped her bag on the foot of the bed and started rooting through it.

She poured some of the coconut oil she'd brought with her into her hands, rubbed them together to heat it, and straddled his hips. Val's head was cradled on his arms, his hair spread out and his eyes closed. He smiled when she leaned forward and brushed his hair out of the way, but he didn't open his eyes.

With long, smooth strokes she spread the oil over his back and shoulders. She started with a light soothing touch, spreading the oil and enjoying the feel of his muscles softening beneath her touch.

"That's it," she murmured as she worked. "Relax for me, baby. I just want to get to know your body better. You seem to know mine extraordinarily well and turnabout is fair play."

"Just remember you said that," he growled.

She laughed. He was relaxing, and she was loving the freedom of touching wherever she wanted. Tenderness welled inside her as she worked the tension out of his neck, then started down his back, digging her fingers into the muscles between his shoulders. Val wasn't a big muscle-bound guy. He was long and lean, with a layer of tight strength throughout. Lethal—that's what he was.

Sliding lower, she worked the middle of his back. Then she was on his ass. God, what an ass. Tight and firm and completely biteable.

She put a little more oil in her hands and started to massage his buttocks. His legs shifted beneath her as she kneaded and squeezed. Remembering what he'd done to her that night in the private party room, she spread his cheeks and ran an oiled thumb over his puckered anus.

A seductive groan echoed through the room and he shivered. Excitement flared deep in her belly and she passed her thumb over the area again before quickly moving down to his thigh.

He hadn't told her to stop. He even seemed to like the sensation her light touch had caused, but she'd felt the slight tensing of his body when she'd touched him the second time. She massaged his left leg, working her thumbs into the muscles of his thigh and continuing down his lightly furred calf. When she touched his foot, he silently jerked it out of her reach.

"Are you ticklish?" Her delight evident in her voice, she reached for his foot again.

Again he jerked it out of her hand the second her fingers touched the bottom of his foot. A growl sounded from the top of the bed and she giggled. "Okay, okay, I won't touch your feet."

She started at his thigh again and massaged the back of his right leg before getting him to turn over. Slowly she worked her way back up his body, pleased to see that while his muscles had become pliant under her hands, his cock stood strong and proud.

She glanced up to see him watching her. With a sultry smile she opened her mouth and took him deep. Feeling the throb of hot blood flowing through him against her tongue ripped a sigh of satisfaction from her throat. He felt so good there, tasted so good. She closed her eyes, intent on taking her time.

One hand cupped his balls and fondled them while she licked the length of his shaft. Her lips formed a tight circle over the smooth head, and she sucked, using her mouth, her tongue, and her hand to stroke his length all at once. There was no urgency, just a languorous loving that felt completely right

His breathing grew harsh and his fingertips brushed against her ears. His balls tightened in her hand and his cock twitched against her tongue. Samair lifted her head and stared at the man beneath her. Her gaze traveled up over his sculpted chest to meet dark eyes full of desire and tenderness.

Firm hands gripped her shoulders, urging her up his body until his hot breath floated over her skin a second before his soft lips brushed hers. She lay stretched out on top of him, their naked bodies pressed together, his cock hot and hard between them as he rolled her to her back.

He tangled his long fingers in her hair, turning her head and slanting his mouth over hers. His hips slipped into the cradle of her thighs and lust coiled low in her belly as they kissed, mouths opening, tongues searching, breath blending.

Valentine filled all of her senses, his flavor slightly musky, his scent that of a man. The strong muscles of his thighs flexed above her, and she pressed against him. His hands gripped her hips, rocking her against him and making her pussy throb in time with her pounding heart.

He moved his hips and his cock thrust home, filling her up and making stars explode behind her eyes. An ecstatic cry leapt from her lips as her inner walls clenched around him, milking him as he pumped slow and steady into her until a rough groan echoed in the room.

He buried his head in her neck, his body trembling above hers, while his warmth flooded her body.

Samair felt the soft press of a kiss on her forehead before the weight of his body shifted and she was snuggled into the curve of his body for the remainder of the night.

28

"What do you mean, you haven't had sex yet?"

It was three days until Samair's fashion show and Joey's tiny apartment had turned into one big fitting room for the afternoon. And, as usual with a room full of women, talk had quickly turned to men and sex.

"What, you've never heard of dating?" Joey glared at Tara.

Joey was enjoying getting to know Mike. Since that first night a week ago when they'd sat up and talked, they'd been on three dates. Each of them fun, entertaining . . . and arousing. The time spent at the end of each date making out without getting off was starting to piss her off.

It messed with her head the way he looked at her like he

wanted to eat her up. The heat they generated when together was stronger than anything she'd ever felt, yet he still held back. It was getting to the point where she was either going to jump him or walk away from him.

"I've heard of dating." Tara looked up from the leather-and-chain-mail contraption in her hands. "I've just never experienced it."

"That's because you have no restraint," Kelly said. "You don't know how to say no on the first date."

Tara bristled. "That's not true. I've said no on the first date plenty of times. Then again, I'm usually saying no to a second date. If I'm interested enough for a second date, I'm interested enough for sex." She gave a giggle and a shrug. "And if I want sex, too, why should I say no?"

"It's worth it."

Joey turned from her own pile of lingerie to Samair's friend Ginger. "What's worth it?"

"Waiting when you find the right guy. My man Jason made me wait a month when we first started seeing each other, but let me tell you, by the time I got that man naked, I was completely in love, and it was the best thing ever." She smiled dreamily. "It still is."

"Yeah, and when you first met Jason you weren't even attracted to him!" Samair poked her old coworker in the ribs. "Beth had to talk you into seeing him again."

"True." The tattooed pixie nodded. "I was a little slow

on the draw with him. It was that nice-guy thing, it threw me off balance a little."

Samair threw an *I told you so* look at Joey, but said nothing. Joey really liked Mike, and it scared her. It was much easier to make her body available than her heart.

As much as they'd talked about Mike over and over, they rarely talked about Sammie's love life. The devil inside Joey prodded, and the words jumped from her mouth. "What about you, Sammie? You've definitely got the bad boy of the group . . . How's it going?"

"Bad boy?" Kelly said from her spot on the sofa.

"You have a new man, Samair?"

Tara planted her hands on her hips and glared. "You've been holding out on us? Spill it, girl. Who's keeping you busy?"

Color flooded Sammie's cheeks and Joey almost felt sorry for her. Almost. There were very few secrets in a group of dancers willing to strut around naked in front of each other, and since they were willing to strut in front of a bar full of people for Samair, a little give and take was a good thing for everyone.

"I've been having some fun with Val for a couple of weeks now."

There was a moment of silence before everyone but Joey responded.

"Val?"

"Valentine Ward?"

"Who's Val?" Ginger was the only one whose jaw wasn't on the floor.

Samair held out a gladiator-style breastplate made from shiny black PVC for Ginger to slip into. "He's the owner of Risqué, and we're not dating, it's just sex."

"So that's why you got asked to do this show at the club. Sweet."

"Fuck that!" Joey glared at Tara. "That's not why she got asked to do the show. She got asked because what she does is freakin' fantastic."

Sometimes women were such bitches to each other. She knew Tara was all pissy because she and Rob were fighting, but Joey wasn't going to let her be a hag to Sammie.

It seemed like Ginger felt the same way because she turned to model the outfit Sammie had just finished buckling up and openly challenged the group. "Look at this outfit and tell me Samair doesn't deserve this show based solely on her talent. This shit isn't exactly run-of-the-mill, you know."

"It's beautiful." Kelly stood and hugged Samair. "She looks like the perfect sex fantasy version of Xena. You totally deserve this show. What I really want to know is . . . how kinky is Val?"

Tara's head popped up through the sweatshirt she was pulling back on. "I want to know . . . how *big* is Val?"

Laughter echoed through the room and the tension was

broken. Sammie blushed and said Val wasn't that kinky at all. "Just potent." She fanned her flushed face.

"I'm telling you all, it's the quiet nice guys that are the closet kinks." Ginger pointed to Joey and the leather corset she'd just finished buckling up. "I'll bet money that if you wear that for that new *nice* guy you're dating, your waiting will be over."

Joey walked over to the mirror and glanced at herself. The corset curved over her hips, cinched her waist with adjustable buckles, and pushed her small breasts together and up into an amazing cleavage.

"Wow." She sighed, running her hands over her torso. She was getting turned on just looking at herself. She swiveled and checked out the backside. With the hourglass look even the basic black leather thong Sammie had given all the girls looked good.

Sammie met her eyes in the mirror and nodded. "I made that one specifically to your measurements. It's yours, Joey, all I ask is that you model it at the show."

A squeal of joy jumped from her lips and she danced around. "Woo hoo, I'm gonna get some action." Mike wasn't going to know what hit him.

Plans started to form in her mind and she ignored Tara's whiny voice. "She gets to keep it? What if someone wants to buy it?"

Before Sammie could answer, the buzzer went off announcing that the guys had arrived. Rob and Jason—dancer Jason, not Ginger's man Jason—had agreed to model for the show as well. She pushed the button that let them into the building and the phone rang. Jeez, everything always happened at once.

She grabbed the phone off the kitchen counter and opened the apartment door a crack so the boys could just walk in. "Hello?"

"Is this Joey Kent, please?"

"This is her." Joey's stomach clenched. She knew that voice already. She'd been waiting for this call. Praying for it.

"Joey, this is Carl Raisen. You did great at the first audition yesterday and I'd like to make an appointment for you to dance for me again. It's between you and two other girls and I'll see each of you individually this time. I have business out of town this weekend but will be back to booking talent for the video next week. Can you make it in on Monday afternoon?"

Blood rushed to her head and she had to squeeze her eyes shut to stay calm. "Of course, I'd love to."

Carl rattled off a time and an address and they said goodbye. When she opened her eyes and hung up the phone, everyone was staring at her. "I got through! I have a final audition for the music video on Monday!"

Strong arms grabbed her from behind and Rob spun her around while everyone cheered. She laughed and chatted with everyone, the room getting smaller and smaller as it filled with people.

"Before we go any further, now that everyone is here, I have something to say." Sammie's voice reached above the chaos. Everyone quieted down and she continued.

"I just wanted to say that I really appreciate all of you agreeing to model for me, especially since I can't pay any of you. So instead of cash payment, I want to give each of you an outfit of your choice. You can pick whichever one you want, and for the dancers, if the lingerie isn't your thing, I can make you a costume that will suit you."

Joey watched her friends cheer and cluster around Sammie for hugs and giggles and her heart swelled. It was a good day, and yet all she could think about was the night to come. Picking up the phone again, she went into the bathroom for some privacy.

The number she dialed was embedded in her memory.

"Hey, baby," she said into the phone when Mike's voicemail came on. "I know you're at work, and that we have plans for later tonight, but I just had to call and tell you I was thinking of you."

29

The music was loud and throbbing, the lights were dim, and the place was filling up. Samair stood at the railing on the top landing looking down on the lower floor of Risqué and pressed a hand to her stomach to still the flutter there.

Heat blanketed her back and warm hands cupped her shoulders. "It's going to be fine." Val kissed the nape of her neck.

"Is that a promise?" she asked without looking at him.

"The show doesn't start for another hour and already we're almost full. The bachelor room *is* full. Everyone is in a good mood; your models are in the office having a grand ol' time. Don't worry."

The last few days had flown by without a chance for she and Val to be alone together. She'd pulled several all-nighters sewing and putting together the half-dozen new designs that were the features of the Fetish and Fantasy show. She'd whipped up several of her other more basic designs as well. The softer, sexier camisoles and lace teddies would help round out the fantasy aspect of the show.

She'd even put together a couple of feathered masks and made a nurse's uniform out of white netting and a few strategically placed scraps of white leather.

The models had been coached so that once the stage and runway part of the show was over, they'd go out into the crowd and chat people up, and sell, sell, sell.

Samair turned, resting her back against the railing and facing Val. Just being near him was calming her nerves. "Thanks for offering the models some incentive. I appreciate it."

"A few bar tabs isn't much to me. It's the least I could do for you." He kissed her forehead.

The least he could do? Samair remembered the fully loaded catering tables in the bachelor room and the flyers plastered all over town. She'd even heard the show promoted on a local radio station that afternoon. He'd done so much already.

Taking a deep breath, she looked up at him. "Why are you doing all this?"

"What do you mean?" His expression never changed. He still looked calm, cool, and collected, but Samair's radar hummed.

"What's in this for you? I mean, you were fucking me before, so it's not sex, and it's not like Risqué needs more business. So what do you get out of putting so much into this?"

Their eyes met and the silence grew.

"Money," he said finally. "Money is what I get. An event like this, where I can charge a lot at the door and I don't have to pay you, or the models, brings a lot of money into the club."

"I don't get it." Samair shook her head. Unable to not touch him, she reached out and rested a hand on his tense biceps. "If it's just about making some money and getting exposure for the club, why didn't you tell me that when I asked you the first time?"

"Sam! You look great, sis. Are you nervous?"

His timing sucked, but Samair was delighted to hear her brother's voice, just the same. She stepped around Val and greeted Brett with a hug. "Nervous, anxious, nauseated, all of the above. Thank you so much for coming!"

"Of course I came. I was planning to come to see what you've been up to anyway—the flyers have been all over the place—so the fact that I can actually help out is a bonus." Brett let her go and held out his hand to Val. "Brett Jones, Sam's brother."

Samair stepped in to finish the introductions. "This is Valentine Ward, Brett. The owner of the nightclub, and my friend."

Val's eyes widened slightly at the introduction, but then he smiled and some of the tension eased from him visibly. "It's a pleasure to meet you, Brett. Samair tells me you're quite the hockey player."

The men started to talk hockey and Samair tuned them out. Val was looking very sexy in his tux, and his presence was exciting, yet comforting. It was nice to have Brett there, too. She'd called Cherish and her parents and told them about the show as well, but the complete lack of interest and understanding in their voices had kept her from actually inviting them.

Surprisingly, when Ginger had shown up, she'd brought not only her man Jason, but Samair's old boss Bethany and her husband, Grant.

"I'm so excited for you, Samair." Bethany had wrapped her in a big warm hug when they'd arrived. "This is fabulous!"

"Thank you. And thank you for coming. How's the baby?"

"Big," she'd laughed. "Big enough that I'll be going back to the boutique soon."

"Only part time," her husband had said as he tucked her against his side.

The love and affection between them was obvious, and when Ginger ushered them away to their table, the adoration in Jason's eyes for her was just as blatant.

Everything was working out better than Samair could've

expected. She had friends and even part of her family around her. The sexy man at her side was pretty damn nice, too, even if there was still so much about him she didn't know.

"Well, Sam, where do you want me?" Brett's voice pulled her out of her thoughts.

"I'm going to check on things in the bachelor room. Once you get your brother organized, check on the models and remind them to get down to the tent by the separate entrance early." Val pressed a small kiss to her temple and rubbed her back comfortingly. "I'll see you there."

Val walked away and Samair's stomach dropped. Brett grinned. "He seems like a good guy. A little older than you, and definitely rough and tough beneath the surface. Mom and Dad will hate him."

Samair shuddered. "Mom and Dad will never meet him, Brett. He's a lover, that's all. Not a boyfriend."

"Uh-huh."

Val found Karl in the bachelor room, schmoozing with the more influential people who had wanted their privacy assured, and were willing to pay handsomely for it.

To him, it was a contradiction that people who were so paranoid about their privacy would come out to a show anyway. Karl had worked his magic though, assuring them that they would have complete privacy from the rest of the club with a private show.

The logistics of giving them a separate fashion show hadn't been easy to figure out. They'd set up a small changing tent just outside the bachelor room's separate entrance on the side of the building, and the models had agreed to do a change out there. Then they'd all go back inside and do the show again, for the general occupants of the bar.

"How's it going in here?" he asked Karl when he found him at the back, watching over the crowd.

"Smooth, buddy. Your staff is keeping the drinks flowing, and the catering is a definite hit."

Val looked over at the tables along the back wall of the room. He'd arranged for buffet style catering and the two end tables were piled high with hot hors d'ocuvres such as poached salmon rounds and crab puffs, along with plates and such. But the middle table was what made it all special.

Centered in the dimly lit area was a long table, the crisp white linen cloth covering it a deep contrast to the dark skinned body stretched out on top of it.

Sushi, sashimi, tempura-battered veggies, and prawns covered the woman's bare flesh. Flower petals of various colors and leafy greens were strategically littered over her breasts and belly, while a small porcelain plate with pickled ginger and wasabi waited in the juncture of her thighs, hiding just enough of her hairless pussy to tease.

"For two hundred bucks a head I figured I'd better come up with something other than free booze for them. Ambrosia Catering promised me that, and I see they delivered."

Karl slapped him on the back.

"All the tickets were sold, so that's some solid coin. Between this and what you make at the front door, you're home free, brother."

"As much as I hate to anticipate . . . I think you're right. Now if we can sell a lot kinky shit, Samair's new business will be off to a great start, too."

"How's she doing?"

Val gave him a look.

"Hey, I like her." Karl grinned. "She seemed pretty smart, she's got a rockin' body, and there's no arguing with her taste in lingerie."

"Speaking of which, you got plans later tonight?"

Karl's eye narrowed. "Not really. Why?"

30

Samair gritted her teeth and let Joey push her out of the ladies room they'd commandeered as a dressing room for the final show. The private showing in the bachelor room had already gone off without a hitch and it was only minutes until the second showing, the one that would take place on the dance floor.

"We're *fine*," Joey said with a gentle push. "You're driving us nuts though, so go sit and watch like the rest of the crowd."

Mike turned from his post outside the change room, and the two exchanged a lingering look. He was there to make sure nobody got in the dancers' way as they strutted to the dance floor, and he grinned when he saw Samair's mutinous expression.

"They're a cocky bunch, aren't they?" he asked.

Samair felt her cheeks flush. "Yes, they are. It's a good thing they know what they're doing." *I hope.*

She looked around the club, at a loss as to where to go until she spotted Bethany waving at her from a few feet away.

"Ready?" she asked when Samair joined their table just as the lights dimmed and the music lowered.

"Not by a long shot."

"Welcome to Risqué, everyone." Val was standing in the middle of the dance floor on the temporary raised stage they'd had put in. "We're normally closed on Sunday nights, but tonight is special. Tonight is the debut show for a local fashion designer who specializes in the naughty and risqué. Her name is Samair Jones, and the label you're all going to want to remember is Trouble. Now please, sit back and enjoy your first look at her new line."

Instead of watching the show, Samair watched the crowd. The dancers strutted their stuff as people nodded and smiled, some oohed and aahed, and a few looked bored. She didn't panic at the bored expressions of one or two; she could see the outfits with a critical eye, and knew they were just what she'd been aiming for.

By the time the six of them did a final walk-through together, people were pointing and everyone was clapping. The models stopped on stage and waved Samair up. Pleasure and pride made her heart race as she stepped on stage with her models and took a bow. Her eyes met Joey's and the two of them grinned like idiots. A dream had just come true, and they both knew it.

She stepped off the stage without saying a word to the crowd. She didn't need to; her designs had spoken for themselves, and the models were making their way through the crowd now to show them off up close.

Bethany rushed up to her as soon as she was on the ground and gave her a big hug. "I knew you loved to play with and alter clothes, Samair, but I had no idea that my shy and quiet salesgirl had so much talent. You did terrific!"

Suddenly Val was at her side, speaking softly. "Fantastic show, babe. So fantastic Karl is swamped in the bachelor room taking orders for Trouble, and Brett is still in there helping him, so we've got no one out here to take orders."

"Have you got a price list?"

Both Samair and Val faced Bethany in surprise.

"What?" she said. "I ran a clothing boutique for a long time, I think I can take some special orders."

Overwhelmed with surprise and appreciation, Samair almost cried. "Really? You don't mind?"

Samair made a quick dash up to Val's office and snatched up a pre-printed price list, and a stack of her business cards for Bethany. She'd just handed them off to her friend and was getting ready to work the crowd when a sullen couple stepped in front of her.

"Well, well, well. Who knew you had it in you?" the bleached blonde said with a smirk.

"Lisa, what are you doing here?" Anger bubbled to life in her gut.

She'd made it a point to retrieve her stuff from the apartment when Lisa was at work, and even though they'd spoken briefly on the phone a few times about the apartment, they hadn't seen each other since the night Samair had walked out.

"We heard about the show and had to come check it out. You know, seeing is believing and all that."

Samair looked at Kevin, standing silent beside Lisa, his embarrassment clear. "I hope you enjoyed the show," she said through gritted teeth and turned to leave.

Only a sharp-clawed hand grabbed her arm and swung her back to see an ugly snarl on Lisa's face. "I know you only got into this kinky stuff in an effort to get Kevin back, but it's not going to work. You can pretend all you want, but we both know you can't give him what he needs."

"First off," Samair said as she jerked her arm out of Lisa's grip. A large presence closed in behind her but she didn't bother to look back. "I've been sewing and designing my own clothes since I was sixteen, which you would know if you'd bothered to be a real friend when we lived together. Secondly, I have no desire to see *either* of you ever again. Therefore, thirdly, anything I get into—kinky or otherwise—has absolutely nothing to do with you."

Lisa's mouth opened but Samair beat her to the punch. She crossed her arms over her chest and spoke firmly. "Save it. Whatever you have to say, I don't want to hear it. If you're not here to enjoy the party, then leave."

"You okay?" Val asked softly from behind her when Lisa and Kevin were out of earshot.

She summoned a smile and spun around to face him. "I'm great. How are you?"

His eyes narrowed. She could see he wanted to push the issue, but before he could say anything another woman appeared to congratulate Samair on a wonderful show. A steady stream of people came up to Samair and she lost track of Val as she mingled, absorbing the energy of the crowd and living in the moment.

The best part of the show for Joey was the fact that Mike had seen it. There had been many, many hot eyes on her throughout the night. First, in the luxurious private room, then out in the club. When the show was over, and she was mingling in the club, letting people see her outfit up close and touch the materials, she did her best to stay focused on the job. To tell them about the outfit, and how to order things, to hand out business cards and rave about all of the clothes she'd been wearing over the years that had been made by the talented Samair Jones. An hour after the show finished, there was finally enough of a lull that she could speak to him.

"One more hour to go, baby. Then I'll give you a very private show."

His smile was rueful. "I have to be at work early, and you have an important audition tomorrow. You need to get some sleep, so it's no good for either of us to stay up all night talking again."

Hurt, frustration, and confusion welled up inside her. But she was strong and independent, and she didn't want him to see just how much his rejection stung. She stretched her lips into a smile and shrugged. "Okay, have a good night then," she said. And walked away.

"Joey," he called after her. But she kept going. Pretending not to hear him, she headed for the bachelor room to do one last go-around. Val had brought in private security for the room, and Mike couldn't follow her. Not that he even tried.

31

The Fetish and Fantasy show was held as a special event on a Sunday night, when Risqué would normally be closed. It worked out well that way because the regular party-all-night crowd wasn't in attendance and when last call was announced at midnight instead of two in the morning, the place was already emptying out.

Samair was flying high on adrenaline and jubilation, floating six inches off the ground as she stood on the top landing saying good night to people as they left. Not only had Brett handed her forty-three orders from the clients in the bachelor room—several of which were orders for more than one item—but Vera, Val's ex wife, had made it a point to make a lunch date with her.

Samair wasn't sure exactly what that was all about. The woman was openly flirtatious and seductive toward her, making it clear she was sexually attracted, but when she'd made the date she'd implied it was about placing a large order from Trouble. Samair had only been with one woman in her life and that was Joey. While she wasn't biased against same-sex relationships, she wasn't interested in one either. Her affair with Joey had been a one-time thing, her curiosity had been sated, and their friendship cemented in it. But deep down, Samair knew she loved cock way too much to go that route again. Especially with Val's ex-wife.

She didn't know what to make of the relationship between Val and Vera, either. She'd seen them talking at one point. Well, Vera had been talking, her head tilted up and her hand on his sleeve in that universal flirtatious way of a woman trying to seduce, while he'd scowled down at her. Just as Samair had started to make her way over to them, Val had leaned in close to say something, then stalked away.

That was when Vera had zeroed in on Samair, and she'd gotten the distinct impression that whatever Val had said to her had set Vera's seduction in motion.

"Don't be such a stranger, Samair." Ginger's voice interrupted her thoughts. Samair snapped back to the present to see Ginger and Bethany, and their respective men, coming toward her.

"We don't have work to hang out at together anymore, so

don't make me hunt you down again," Ginger said, pulling her into a fierce hug.

"I won't—be a stranger that is—although your timing on this last hunt was absolutely perfect." Bethany reached over and hugged her, too. "Thank you so much for coming, I'm sorry I had to put you to work."

"Are you kidding?" Grant laughed. "You made her night!"

Beth smacked him playfully, but gave Samair a sincere smile. "He's right. I enjoyed every minute of it. Sexy and erotic you definitely did, and the workmanship and love you put into making the clothes is obvious. It was easy to sell."

A store of her own. Wow. For the first time ever, the concept wasn't completely unrealistic. Joey joined them then, now dressed in jeans and a faded T-shirt with Danskin scrawled across her breasts.

She exchanged hugs and good-byes then they watched the two couples leave together. Next to her, Joey let out a heavy sigh.

"What's wrong? You wish you'd gone dancing now?" The other dancers and models had left about half an hour earlier, on their way to a different club to do some dancing.

"Nothing's wrong. The night was a complete success for you. I'm thrilled."

The grin Joey flashed her didn't quite reach her eyes, and Samair almost growled her impatience. "Don't bullshit me, Joey. Something's wrong, now tell me."

"Nothing," she mumbled, ducking her head. "It's just Mike."

Comprehension dawned. "Still no lovin' happening?"

"I thought for sure after tonight he'd be ready to go, but he's not into it. He has to work early."

"Well, he does have a day job," Samair reminded her gently. "Maybe the last all-nighter you two pulled was too much for him."

"We *talked* all night then!"

"Still, it was all night. Not all of us can get by on four or five hours of sleep like you can, honey."

"I don't get it, Sammie. He wanted to date, so we dated. We've gone out four times, movies, coffee, dinner, and still I get nothing more than a long kiss goodnight. After watching me strut around this club in less than a bra and underwear all night, he still isn't interested in sex? He's not interested period." She straightened her shoulders. "From now on, he's just a friend. That's the way he wants things, so I'm moving on."

Samair saw the hurt and the stubbornness in her friend's mulish expression and gave up. There was no talking to Joey when she'd made up her mind about something.

Instead, she just tugged her into a hug. She pulled back slightly and pressed her forehead to Joey's, staring deep into her eyes. "I love you."

"I know." Joey kissed her quickly. "Thank you."

They pulled apart and she smacked Joey on the butt as she walked away. "See you later, brat."

The club was almost empty. A few stragglers milled about. Kelsey, the cute Goth bartender, was shutting down the bar while the waitresses wiped the last of the tables clean and Mike urged the final few people toward the stairs. She couldn't see Val on the floor anywhere, and after a quick look in the office with no results, she headed for the bachelor room.

She smiled at Marc, the bouncer guarding the door under the stairs, and went in. The bartender was gone, the guests were gone, and the catering tables were all cleared. Karl stood near the rear exit with the woman who had been the human centerpiece on the catering table. Her eyes finally found Val seated in an overstuffed armchair. Sitting across from him was a good looking guy who she'd never met. Val saw her watching and waved her over.

"Samair, this is Jonathan. Jonathan, this is my friend, and the woman behind all the lingerie you saw tonight, Samair."

He was even better looking up close. He also looked to be approximately thirty, younger than she'd first thought. He had midnight black hair cut short and a darker complexion that made his light blue eyes stand out eerily.

"Hello, Jonathan, I hope you enjoyed the show." Samair smiled and perched on the arm of Val's chair.

"It was very well done. I placed an order for several items.

Val assured me that shipping them would not be a problem." Those piercing eyes ran over her lightly and a tingle of arousal roused low in her belly.

Val put a hand on her thigh and she glanced down at him. He didn't smile but his eyes held the beginnings of a dark hunger that never failed to remind her that he was the big bad wolf, ready to eat her up.

Her pulse skipped and her body warmed, softening and readying itself for his possession. Dragging her eyes from him, she focused on the new man across from them. "You're not from Vancouver?"

He shook his head, a small smile playing at the corners of his mouth. "I visit often, but my job requires a lot of travel. One of the purchases on my order is for a local friend who will make herself available to you for fittings and such. I'll e-mail the measurements and specifics to you for the others."

Karl came up to them and clapped a hand down on Val's shoulder. "I'm out of here, buddy. I'll be back tomorrow to go over things with you." The two men shook hands before he leaned down and placed a gentle kiss on Samair's cheek, surprising her. "You were a hit. Great job."

He nodded at Jonathan and left through the rear entrance.

Samair gave herself a mental headshake. Being the only female with three very attractive and mesmerizing men, if only for a moment, had her juices flowing. Trying to ignore the direction her thoughts were traveling in, she smiled at Jonathan and continued their conversation. "It sounds like everything is worked out. I'm pleased you found some things you liked."

His smile grew and he gave Val a small nod. "There's a lot to like."

Val's hand slipped beneath the slit in her skirt and higher on her thigh. She gasped, her gaze flying to his.

"You mentioned once that two men, focused completely on you, was one of your fantasies. I told you I could make all your fantasies come true." His intense gaze burned into her, seeing everything, telling nothing. "If you're willing."

32

Samair held on tight to Val as he directed the Harley toward his place. There had been very little talking between them since she'd uttered the words, "I'm willing."

They'd left the bar then. Jonathan got into a cab while Val had let his staff know he was leaving.

The rumbling vibrations of the bike between her thighs kept her body at such a fever pitch that when Val stopped at a red light, she let her hands slip forward from his hips to his thighs. His muscles flexed beneath her hands and the heat of him soaked through her palms and into her blood.

A threesome. Not just any threesome, but one with two men. One of them Val.

Too many times to count, she'd used the fantasy of two

men completely centered on her to reach orgasm. She'd used it when masturbating, as well as when she'd been with other lovers. She'd never used fantasies to get off when she was with Val. Maybe it was because with him she didn't need to fantasize. Right from the first night she met him, everything he did for her was a dream come true. The fantasy comment about sex with a stranger had been a throwaway at the time. Something that had popped into her head and out of her mouth. Until then she'd never really given her fantasies much thought. Not the sexual ones, nor the career ones. And here she was riding on the back of a Harley after her first fashion show—a successful fashion show—on her way to experience yet another fantasy come true.

She pressed closer to Val, squeezing his hips with her legs and once again slipping her hands to the inside of his thighs just as the bike rolled to a stop. She climbed off the bike and he followed, silently relieving her of her helmet before taking her by the hand and leading her into his apartment.

Once inside, he sandwiched her body up against the wall.

"You test my control every time you touch me," he muttered before taking her mouth. His tongue swept in and took complete control.

Samair's mind shut down and her body took over. Her fingers thrust into his silky hair, dislodging the elastic tie as his hands grabbed her ass and lifted. She wrapped her legs around him and felt his hardness press against her core. His hips thrust against her and her insides tightened.

"Yes," she gasped. "Val—"

The doorbell rang and they both froze.

Their eyes met and Samair bit her bottom lip.

"Tell me you want this. Both of us."

"I want this," she whispered.

He pressed a soft kiss to her lips. "I'll take care of you. I'll make it good for you." Then he pulled back, ran his hands through his hair, and went to open the door.

Without looking at either of the men, Samair walked to Val's bedroom. She took her coat off as she walked and she heard the men behind her speaking in low tones.

Part of her knew that if things didn't get started right away, she might back out. Yes, she wanted this, but part of her also worried that if she went through with it, there could never be anything more than sex with Val. What man would want to be in a serious relationship with a woman he'd shared?

In that moment Samair realized that she actually wanted a serious relationship with Val. Uncertainty hit her hard and a minute trembling began in her muscles.

Val stepped into the bedroom and she met his fiery gaze. There was no disgust or revulsion in his eyes, but there was something infinitely stronger than basic lust.

Holding her gaze, he stepped forward and brushed the backs of his fingers down her cheek. "Okay?"

She nodded. He trailed his hand down her neck and across the swell of her breast exposed by the low neckline of her wraparound top. His hand followed the seam between her breasts and across her belly to the knot at her hip. He undid the knot, and at the same time she became aware of another presence behind her.

Jonathan.

While Val opened her blouse, a second set of male hands skimmed lightly over her hips to the waist of her skirt.

Samair closed her eyes and let the breath rush out of her lungs. She shoved her trepidation aside and welcomed the sensations that swamped her as two sets of hands removed her clothing. Surprisingly, even with her eyes closed she knew which hands were Val's and which were Jonathan's.

Everything took on a dreamlike quality. When she was completely naked, Jonathan's arms encircled her, pulling her close so that her back was cradled against his front. His hands skimmed over her torso from collarbone to belly button, and he pressed a soft kiss to the sensitive spot beneath her ear.

"Open your eyes, darlin', and watch your man."

Samair struggled to lift her heavy eyelids only to be rewarded with the sight of Val slowly and methodically stripping.

Jonathan cupped her breasts, his fingers plucking at the rigid nipples while his teeth nibbled along her neck. She could feel his hard-on pressing against her backside and she wiggled her hips, pressing back into him. Val shed the last of his clothes and came toward her. Jonathan stood his ground and Val stepped right up, pressing his nakedness against hers, slipping his hands around to cup and squeeze her bottom.

She stood pressed tightly between the two hard bodies, one completely clothed, the other completely naked, their hands encircling her, touching her, skimming over her skin. Jonathan nipped and nibbled on one side of her neck and Val licked and kissed the other. Pleasure hit every nerve ending she had, and with an ecstatic groan, her knees buckled and she went over the edge.

Val had picked her up and carried her to the bed. He laid her down and stretched out next to her, his elbow bent and his head resting in his hand, while she caught her breath. Then Jonathan was on her other side, one hand on her belly, his eyes smiling into hers.

Languorous pleasure flowed through her as each man cupped a breast. Val bent forward, his lips covering a breast as he sucked a nipple into his mouth. She moaned, arching into him. He flicked the nipple with his tongue then nipped at it sharply before soothing it with soft kisses. He stretched and started to give the other breast the same treatment. This time Samair's moan was caught by Jonathan's mouth as he brushed his lips across hers. His tongue snuck out and licked at her lips, teasing her before slanting over and taking possession.

His flavor was strong and masculine, with a hint of mint.

Just as she was registering the difference in his flavor from Val's, hands shifted on her body, reaching between her legs to stroke her sex, while other hands cupped her breasts.

Closing her eyes, she let herself go. Her hands reached out, stroking whatever she could reach, as Val's mouth replaced his hand between her thighs and Jonathan took over teasing her breasts.

Fingers invaded her pussy, and Val's mouth fastened on her clit, sucking, teasing, his tongue circling. Muscles flexed beneath her hands; her fingertips tangled in Val's hair and speared through Jonathan's shorter style. Suddenly, her body tensed and another orgasm rolled over her.

Val felt Samair's cunt spasm around his fingers as he sucked on her clit. Warm wetness flooded his hand and he lapped it up, loving the musky scent and taste of her desire.

Her legs shifted restlessly on the mattress next to him and he smoothed his hands over them as he pulled away. His dick was throbbing and he thought of entering her right then and there. But this night was for her, not him.

He backed off a bit, leaving the bed to stand aside and catch his breath, get himself back under control. Jonathan glanced his way, a question in his eyes, but Val nodded, giving his okay to continue.

They'd talked in the bachelor room about how things

would go if Samair did indeed want to go through with the threesome. They'd agreed that Val was in charge, and Samair was the center of attention.

It was to be all about pleasing her.

But despite her breathy sighs and passionate moans, as he watched Jonathan stretch out over the top of Samair, he had the sudden urge to growl "Stop."

It felt too much like they were all making love instead of having sex, and Val's gut clenched. He wanted to be the only man she made love to.

With precise movements, he went to the top of the bed and took Samair's hands, pinning them to the mattress. Her eyes flew open and snapped straight to his.

"Does it feel good, baby?" Val spoke softly.

He lay down next to her, watching as Jonathan followed the same path Val had taken. His head burrowed between Samair's thighs as his hands roamed over her legs, her waist, and her ass. He lifted her to get a better angle while he licked her pussy.

Val pinned her wrists with one hand and used his other to play with her nipples. He rolled them between thumb and forefinger, he tugged at them, he flicked them, delighting in the gasps she made. Her hips rolled and she lifted her legs. "Is Jonathan good at eating pussy? Do you like that? Having one man between your legs and another playing with your tits?"

She moaned, her head tossing side to side. "I want . . . I . . . you."

"What, baby? You need to tell me what you want. Anything and it's yours." He licked up the side of her neck, enjoying the salty goodness.

"You . . . I want to touch you." She panted, tugging at her wrists.

He loosened his grip and one of her hands immediately found his hip. She clawed at his ass and muttered some more until he lifted onto his knees so she could grab his cock.

Jonathan, sensing a change of pace, lifted his head and shifted his body. He reached for the condoms he'd thrown on the foot of the bed when he'd taken his clothes off and ripped a foil package open while meeting Val's gaze.

Again, Val nodded. Part of him wanted to stop Jonathan. He wanted to be the one to take her, to claim her as his own. But even more than that, he wanted to please her.

Her hand tightened on his cock, pulling him closer and making it hard for him to think at all. Samair's eyes were open and begging him silently. "What, baby? What do you want?"

Her tongue darted out and swept across that full bottom lip of hers and his dick jerked in her hand. "You. I want you." Her head lifted off the bed and she tried to reach him with her mouth.

With a quick move he flipped her over, getting on his knees

in front of her. Jonathan grabbed her hips and got on his knees behind her. Val cupped her cheek, running his thumb över the smoothness as their eyes met and she opened her mouth. His heart slammed against his ribs and his throat tightened as he guided her forward to take him between her lips.

The moment her mouth closed around him, they both moaned, the vibrations of the sounds she made ripping through his cock and settling in his chest. She sucked gently and started to move, but he gripped her shoulders and held her still. Jonathan gripped her hips and Val felt her body tense for a moment as he entered her from behind.

Samair tensed for a second as she adjusted to being so full. Jonathan's cock wasn't as thick as Val's, but he was a fair size, and long enough that when she started to rock between the two men, she could feel him nudging her magic spot deep within. She began to rock faster, loving the tender feel of Val's hands in her hair and Jonathan's on her hips. The men let her set the pace, remaining still for her. She sucked harder on Val's cock, feeling it throb as his fingers tightened against her scalp. She opened her eyes and looked up to see him watching her with such intensity that everything in her tightened. Her heart pounded and her pussy clenched.

Jonathan's hands tightened and he started to move with her. Matching her rhythm, his cock shafted her deeper with each move. Her breasts bounced with each thrust and one of Val's hands left her head, reaching around to cup her sensitive flesh and tug on her nipple. With each squeeze and tug, a jolt of pleasure shot directly to her cunt.

She closed her eyes, struggling to breathe, and her insides tightened once again. She was so close to coming, overwhelmed by the sensations of two cocks, two sets of hands, the feel of their eyes on her as she took them both, but she didn't want to come. She wanted this to last. Their groans and sighs of pleasure and the wet sucking sounds coming from both Samair's mouth and her pussy filled the room as they fucked her. Joy filled her as the pace picked up and it became apparent that both men were fighting for control over their bodies as well.

All of Samair's muscles tensed as Val's grip on her hair tightened and his cock hit the back of her throat. At the same time, another cock was hitting deep inside her pussy. She was getting hammered from both ends, and just when she thought things couldn't get any better, something brushed her rear entrance. Her eyes flew open and she moaned, her body jerking at the sensations that ricocheted through her.

Jonathan's thumb brushed over the puckerhole again, gently circling then pressing against her, and she couldn't hold back anymore. She roughly pulled her mouth away from Val's cock and screamed as an orgasm ripped through her.

Slowly coming back to reality, she was aware of Jonathan's low groan as his cock jerked inside her and her body clenched, milking him. She lifted heavy eyelids and saw Val directly in front of her, stroking his cock and watching her with a tenderness she'd never seen before. Her lips spread into a naughty grin and she lifted her face to him. "Mark me," she commanded softly. "Mark me as yours."

His eyes widened and emotion flared in his dark eyes. He pumped his cock and she stared deep into his gaze when his roar of satisfaction echoed in the room and hot come jetted from him to blanket her neck and shoulders.

Heavy silence filled the room as everybody struggled to regain their composure. Samair collapsed on the bed, her eyes closed. The mattress shifted beneath her as both men got off. She heard them speak in low voices over the running water in the bathroom as she drifted on a cloud of wicked satisfaction.

The bed shifted again and she cracked an eye open. Jonathan stretched out next to her, one arm laying over her belly, his body cuddling close. Val knelt on the bed next to her. He leaned down and wiped a warm wet facecloth over her neck and shoulders, gently cleaning her up. She smiled softly at him as he folded the cloth before nudging her legs apart and running the cloth over her swollen sex.

When he stood to go back to the washroom, she called his name. He looked at her and she turned on her side, spooning her back against Jonathan and holding her arm out for Val.

He set the dirty cloth on the nightstand and lay down in front of her. His hand settled on her hip, their feet tangled, and they just looked at one another.

Samair had worried that having him see her with another man would make him lose respect for her, make him not want her anymore. Instead, she saw something like love in his gaze, and her heart swelled.

She closed her eyes on a sigh and drifted off to sleep on the thought that yet another dream had come true.

33

Val watched Samair sleep and his heart thumped against his chest. Her dark eyelashes lay against her smooth fair skin, a slight flush still colored her cheeks, and her lips parted slightly as a delicate snore escaped.

She was beautiful.

When he'd decided to make this fantasy happen for her, he'd intended for Karl to be the second man. They'd shared women before, and he was the natural choice since Samair knew him. But when he'd brought up the subject earlier that night at the club, Karl had turned him down. "It's not a good idea for us to share a woman you plan on keeping around, buddy."

At first he'd thought Karl was saying a threesome was

a bad idea, period. But instead, Karl had introduced him to Jonathan, a friend from out of town. And now, as he fought the urge to forcibly remove Jonathan's arm from around Samair's waist, he understood why.

Sharing Samair had been harder than he'd thought, and he was thankful now that it had been with a man that neither of them would ever see again. As if sensing Val's thoughts, Jonathan's arm lifted from around Samair's waist.

Val watched as the man kissed her cheek and eased from the bed to dress. Val slipped from Samair's side and stepped into his slacks as well, doing up the zipper but leaving them unbuttoned as he walked Jonathan to the door.

"Thank you," he said, offering the other man his hand.

Jonathan smiled, the look in his eyes almost wistful. "It was my pleasure. You have a good woman there. I'd hang on to her if I were you."

"I plan to." The immediate response was instinctive, and, Val realized, true.

With that Val let Jonathan out and returned to his room. He shucked his pants and crawled onto the bed, pulling a quilt over them as he laid down and wrapped his arms around Samair. He buried his face in her hair and breathed deeply.

He couldn't deny it any longer—Samair was more than a playmate to him. He knew when it had happened, too. That first night when she'd come over, things between them had shifted. Even though they'd both said they only wanted a casual sex thing, the emotion and passion between them had made them both liars.

Deep down, he knew that she'd gotten to him in a way no woman ever had, not even Vera. And, strangely enough, he was happy about it.

He just hoped she was, too.

34

Samair awoke slowly, her body relaxed as if pure pleasure were flowing through her veins instead of blood. She didn't open her eyes though. Instead, she remained as she was, on her back, legs spread, and concentrated on the feel of Val's mouth on her sex.

His hands cradled her butt, holding her still as he licked her slit from one end to the other. A breathy moan escaped her and the muscles in her legs twitched. His tongue nudged between her swollen pussy lips and burrowed its way to her center. He thrust it in and out, his face nuzzling closer. The roughness of his morning stubble rubbed deliciously against her ass as his teeth scraped over her clit.

Her fingers dug into the bed sheets, the knot of arousal

low in her belly, tightening to the point that she started to whimper. His tongue left her entrance and traveled up to flick at the senstitve nub and she rolled her hips, pressing against him. Taking the hint, Val's mouth opened and he sucked her clit between his lips, flicking it rapidly with his tongue and sending her into orbit with a victorious cry.

He crawled up her body and slid inside her smoothly. When she opened her eyes she returned his smile. "Good morning." She wrapped her arms around his neck and her legs around his waist.

No more words were spoken. None were needed as he pumped into her. Moments later, when his back arched and his every muscle trembled, she held him close, murmuring encouragement and welcoming his pleasure, even without her own.

They didn't talk about the night before, or the events of the morning as they rose and showered. Instead, their conversation centered on the Fetish and Fantasy show, and the results of it.

"It was certainly a success for me. I hope it was worthwhile for Risqué."

Val nodded as he buttered a bagel that had just popped up from the toaster. "It was good. I won't know exactly how good until I do the numbers this morning, but I think it was a complete success."

Something niggled at the back of her mind and she swallowed the bite of bagel she'd been chewing. "Are you going to tell me what that means? A complete success?"

His shoulders tensed beneath his T-shirt and Samair waited. When he made his way across the small kitchen and settled into the chair across from her she could almost see the wheels turning in his head. Would he trust her? Would he finally share more than his body with her?

Her heart pounded and she bit her lip, holding her breath. He looked up, his smile not quite reaching his eyes. "It means lots of money for us both."

She tried not to let her disappointment show as she got up to put her plate in the sink. Instead, she bent and brushed her lips against his. "Let's go find out how we did, then."

They made a quick stop at the apartment so Samair could change. She chose a pair of jeans and a stretchy knit top that would show off her cleavage. She read Joey's note about her audition that day and said a quick prayer for her friend that it went off without a hitch before jogging down the stairs to where Val waited.

She stepped outside the building and froze. Val straddled his bike, dressed in his biker leathers, chaps and everything. His helmet rested on his thigh and his profile was to her as he watched a woman herd three kids into a car across the parking lot.

He was the complete and total fantasy, a man who had

made her dreams come true. But she had to face the fact that she was nothing more than entertainment to him. Sure, he treated her well. He probably even liked her. But when it came down to the wire, he only trusted her with his body, and she was just starting to realize that she wanted more than that from a man.

More than that from him.

Sucking a deep breath into her lungs, she strode over to him and got on the back of his bike for what would probably be the last time. Self-preservation told her it was almost time to say good-bye to him.

Val sat behind his desk trying to hide his frustration from Samair. He'd gone over the numbers while she'd boxed up the lingerie that had been left behind the night before. She'd been quiet all morning, but he was glad for her company just the same. Having her there reminded him that he'd built Risqué up from nothing, and it wasn't over yet. Even if he didn't have enough to cover the loan. He had three more days, and he wasn't giving up.

"Well, people, how goes it?" Karl strode into office, his question lighthearted but the look he gave Val serious.

Samair bounded across the floor and threw her arms around Karl in a big hug. "It was a great success. Thank you so much for all of your help, Karl. You're a sweetheart."

Karl looked stricken. "Don't spread that around," he said with a laugh. He looked at Val over Samair's shoulder and his lips tightened when Val shook his head.

"Look at you, all shiny and handsome in a suit and tie." Samair brushed her hands over Karl's shoulders and Val bit back a smartass comment. This was his brother, the man who could've been in bed with them the night before, but said no because he knew Val better than he knew himself. There was no reason for jealousy.

"It's the day job. They expect me to be respectable."

A shrill ringing pierced through the room and Samair jumped. She spun around and tugged her phone out of her backpack while Karl stepped forward and spoke quietly. "Are you sure you didn't make enough?"

Val nodded. "I'm sure." He watched as the color drained from Samair's face.

"How much are you short?"

"Samair?" He ignored Karl and stood, moving around his desk. "What's wrong?"

"Joey? Joey, calm down, sweetheart. Tell me what's wrong."

Samair's panicked baby blues looked at him as she spoke into the phone. "Where are you? No, no, stay there, I'll be right there. Don't do anything."

She snapped the phone shut and looked at him. "Joey's in trouble. I need to get downtown. *Now.*"

"I'll drive," Karl said as the three of them strode from the office.

Val struggled to control his own emotions as he boosted Samair into Karl's pickup and climbed in behind her. Samair told Karl where to go and started to tell them what was happening.

"You remember that producer guy who gave her his card in the club and said he wanted her to audition? She went and danced for him, then last week she got a callback. Today was her callback. I don't know what happened, but she was crying and babbling and sounded pretty freaked." She looked at Val. "If that bastard hurt her, I'll kill him."

Karl got them downtown in less than five minutes. He pulled up to the curb in front of a coffee shop and they saw Joey pacing back and forth, her arms folded across her stomach.

All of them jumped out of the truck, but Samair was the first to reach her. She grabbed Joey by the shoulders, forcing her to stop her pacing and face them. "What happened?"

Val saw the handprint on her cheek and rage started to boil up inside him.

"He wanted a . . . a lap dance. He said that the scene in the video was a like a love scene in sha-shadows, and that it would be a lap dance thing, so he needed me to give him one to show I could do it." She gasped out the story, her hands visibly shaking in Samair's grip. "I . . . did it, Sammie.

I wanted the job, so I started to give him a lap dance. Not naked. I wouldn't strip, but you know . . ."

"I know. Shhh, baby. I know." Samair rubbed her cold hands, trying to get circulation going for Joey again, trying to warm her. But Joey wasn't done with her story yet.

As she told them what happened, a familiar calm settled over Val.

"But he kept telling me to get closer, to touch him. He wanted a real one, and when I started to back away, he grabbed me. He grabbed me by the arms and pushed me back on his desk. He put his hand under my skirt and when I tried to stop him he, he slapped me! The bastard slapped me and I kneed him in the balls. Hard, Sammie. I nailed the fucker good."

"Good girl."

"I ran then. And he was screaming about suing me. Charging me with assault and how it would be my word against his, and I was just some stripper slut so nobody would believe me."

Karl met Val's look and nodded. They'd heard enough. He stepped forward, putting his hands on Samair's shoulders as she hugged Joey to her. "Where's his office, sweetheart?"

Joey pointed up the street. "The door that goes upstairs over the record store."

"You girls get in the truck and wait for us. We'll be right back."

Samair looked at him, searching his gaze, then she nodded and guided Joey to the truck without a word.

He spun on his heel and Karl swung into step at his side. They both knew what needed to be done, and they were ready, willing, and eager to do it. Val pulled open the door Joey had pointed to and they jogged up the stars. Val opened the flimsy door at the top that had RAISEN PRODUCTIONS stenciled on it. There was an empty desk in the front room and Val heard shuffling and muttered curses from the next room. He turned to Karl. "Watch the door. Don't let anyone in; this won't take long."

The door shut behind him and he stalked to the second room. "Carl Raisen?" he asked when he saw the little weasel with his eyes closed, stretched out on an overstuffed sofa, muttering to himself.

"What do you want?" He swung his legs over the side and sat up, still hunched over. Good, Joey had kneed the bastard hard enough that he was still feeling it.

"You made a couple of mistakes, and I'm here to see that you never repeat them." He spoke softly as he stepped into the room and pulled the asshole up by the lapel of his cheap suit.

"Hey, hey, man!" The guy's hand flew up, grabbing at Val's, trying to break free. "I don't know you. You got the wrong guy, dude."

"I'm not your dude, and I don't have the wrong guy." His

patience wore thin and Val lashed out, breaking Raisen's nose. The crack echoed through the room and blood spurted.

"Fuck man! What the hell? I'm gonna sue your ass."

Val hit him again. "Shut the fuck up and listen to me. You aren't going to sue me, and you're not going to sue that little dancer who brought you to your knees, either, you get me?" He hit him in the kidneys this time and let the guy fall.

"Okay, okay," he cried out, hands over his head. "It's over, it's done. I'll forget about her."

"Not just her, you little bastard. If I ever hear of you and your little casting couch scam again and I will make sure you're never able to piss without a doctor's help. After today, you'll still be in one piece, but if you ever set foot inside any of the Vancouver nightclubs again, that'll change. In fact, it might be best if you just leave town, period. You hear me?"

Raisen looked up at Val, his pain-filled eyes begging. "Okay, I'll go. I promise."

"Good." Val smiled grimly and hit him again and again, letting his rage fuel his strength until the bastard was a pitiful heap on the floor.

35

Joey felt like an idiot.

A stupid, ignorant, desperate loser. She'd known when she went into the Raisen Production office that something was off. There was no one else in the office and no dance space. Big hints that something wasn't what it seemed, but she'd pushed on, determined to prove to herself that she was more than a second-class dance instructor who shook her ass at night for nothing.

She'd needed that video gig. Needed it to keep her spirit going, to keep the dream alive. Sammie was well on her way to having her dream coming true, and she'd only been chasing it, really chasing it, for less than a month.

Plus she had a great man who so obviously cared for her.

Jealousy is an ugly thing, and something Joey normally prided herself on not feeling, but the night before she couldn't stop it from rising in her throat when Mike had turned her down *again*, and it was stuck there now.

He'd called her before he'd gone to bed, but she hadn't answered. He'd called three times before Joey had left for her audition, and when she got home, after she'd taken a hot shower and crawled into bed, Sammie had told her that he'd called again.

"He really wants to see you, Joey," Samair said, bringing her a cup of chamomile tea. "I think he knows you're mad at him after last night."

"I'm not mad."

"Then why won't you return his calls? He might be just the thing to make you feel better right now."

"How would you know?" she muttered. She hadn't meant to say it, but the words were out her mouth before her brain had engaged.

Sammie gave her a sharp look, but spoke carefully. "I don't *know*. I just thought maybe if he came over he might help you feel better."

"I don't want to see him."

A guilty look flashed across Sammie's face and Joey's gut rolled. "Sammie?"

"He sounded really desperate when you were in the shower and I told him we were home for the night. He didn't say anything but I got the feeling he was on his way over."

She groaned and buried her head in the pillow. "Damn it, Sammie. Why didn't you mind your own business?"

There was no response except the shifting of the bed as Sammie got up to leave the room. Joey's throat tightened and she forced herself to swallow. She didn't mean to hurt her friend. She just couldn't seem to stop the words from tumbling from her lips.

Wiping away the tears that had started to leak from her eyes, she got out of bed and went to the kitchen. "I'm sorry," she said to Sammie, who was quietly putting the dishes away. "I'm just feeling a little out of sorts after this afternoon and I took it out on you."

Sammie turned from the cupboard and met Joey's stare. "I think there's more to it than that." She planted her hands on her hips. "You want to tell me what's really got you upset?"

Before she could stop herself, her resentment swelled and the words started pouring out. "Everything is always so fucking easy for you. It always has been and it always will be. You complain about your family not letting you be you, but your brother was at the party last night, totally supporting you and helping out. You lose your job and end up with your dream career; you find your boyfriend fucking around and you end up with a man ten times better who will do anything for you. It's just not fair!"

Sammie stepped forward, placing her hands on the breakfast bar that separated them, and leaned closer. Joey saw hurt and anger in the blue eyes that were swimming in tears, but she spoke softly. "My life is far from perfect. My family still has secrets, and one fashion show is only the first step in my dream career. As for Val, he'll only do anything for me if it involves getting naked." Samair shook her head. "But this isn't about me, it's about you. It's about you being scared to let anyone close. Especially a man. Have you ever realized that the reason you're so determined to get Mike to sleep with you is because you use sex to keep people away from your heart?"

"I don't use sex, I enjoy it," Joey spit out. "And it's a damn good thing, too, because it seems to be the only thing that will help me get what I want out of life."

"Now you're talking shit."

"What do you know? You're the one who men want to be with. You're the one they'll throw parties for, or beat up men for. Not me. I'm the one they want a lap dance from."

"Val didn't beat up that guy today for me, honey. He did that for you."

"He was only there for you. Him and his friend. Only you would show up with *two* knights in shining armor. I'd be lucky to get one."

Samair threw up her hands. "That's enough! Can the fucking pity party, Joey! I don't know if you're PMSing on top of the rough day or what, but you are so far out there that you could spit on Mars. Open your fucking eyes. Val and Karl were there because you called *me*. Mike doesn't want a lap dance from you, and you can bet your ass he would've been there to kick the shit out of that bastard today if you'd called him. But you didn't. Do you even know why you didn't call him?"

Discomfited, Joey shrugged. Some of what Sammie said made sense. "Mike doesn't want anything from me."

"I think you know that's not true. I think you know, deep down, that this guy might be the one for you, and that scares you stupid."

Before Joey could say anything else, the door buzzer rang. Sammie went over and answered it. When Mike's voice came over the intercom she stared at Joey with raised eyebrows. "Well? Should I tell him to go away, or are you going to give him, and yourself, a chance at what might be a good thing?"

Joey nodded and tried to speak. Her mouth opened but only a squeak came out. She cleared her throat and tried again. "Let him in, please."

Sammie pushed the button to let Mike up, then grabbed her jacket off the hook by the door. She opened the door and spoke over her shoulder. "I've got nowhere else to go, so I will be back tonight, but I'll give you a few hours alone."

Then she was gone.

Joey knew she'd hurt her best friend, and she wanted to go after her, but as she stood frozen, staring at the doorway, Mike filled it.

"Hi," he said.

"Hi." She ran a nervous hand through her hair. She was wearing bright blue pajamas with little white bunnies all over them, no makeup, and her hair still damp from her shower. If the sight of her didn't scare him away, he was a bigger idiot than she was. "Come on in."

He closed the door behind him. She turned away, going to sit on the love seat, knowing he would follow.

"What's going on, Joey?" Concern made his green eyes darken as he sat down next to her. "Why'd you walk away from me last night and why won't you return my calls?"

She debated what to say. She didn't want to tell him about the audition fiasco and have him see her for the fool she was, but she desperately wanted to curl up against his massive chest and let him comfort her.

Instead, she straightened her spine and looked him in the eye. All or nothing. "I want to know what's wrong with me. Why you don't want to have sex with me? I know I don't look so good right now, but you've seen what I have to offer."

"That's what this is about?" He scrubbed a hand over his face and glared at her. "I thought you were sick or hurt or something, and this is because I want it to mean something when we make love?"

"When we make love?"

"I thought I made it clear to you that I didn't want to just fuck. Not that that doesn't have it's place, too, but I really like you, Joey, and I thought you liked me, too."

Confusion hit her and she ducked her head. "I do like you."

"Then why are you in such an all-fired hurry? I'm hoping we'll be together a while, so we can take things slow, do things right."

She shifted her weight, inching closer and trying to ignore the urge to climb right into his lap.

"Joey, it's true you're beautiful, and so sexy you make me hard with nothing more than a smile. But you have more to offer than a hot body or just looking good on my arm. What makes me want you is *you*. You're always so full of energy and laughter and life. Your obvious love of life is what makes you special. Not your face or your body, or even the way you dance." He shook his head, his eyes just a little sad. "I think you're special, and you deserve to be treated that way. Don't you?"

By the time he was done speaking tears were streaming down her cheeks and she couldn't fight her natural urge anymore. She climbed onto his lap, wrapped her arms around him and buried her face in his neck.

He liked *her*!

36

Samair walked around for a while. It was early still, and it was a nice clear night. The air was crisp and cool, and it felt wonderful on her heated cheeks.

There was a school four blocks from the apartment, and Samair headed there as she tried to bury the hurt Joey had caused. She knew it was unintentional, that Joey was hurting from the situation with Mike and the shitty audition, and she'd been lashing out at whoever was closest. She knew Joey hadn't meant to wound her.

But she also knew that those words had come from somewhere.

The schoolyard was empty and Samair made her way to the playground. One set of swings had the thick canvas seats and Samair was glad. She'd always loved to swing, but she couldn't fit her wide hips into the wooden-seated ones on the next set. She settled in and kicked off, still thinking about Joey.

What she'd said was partially true, too. Like the energy that came from deep within that got her noticed when she wanted, she knew that things had sort of come easy for her. No, that's not true. Things hadn't come easy for her. Sure, it might seem like she'd always gotten what she wanted, but in all honesty, she worked hard for everything. Nothing had been handed to her. And no one but her knew just how hurtful being the black sheep in a family full of golden-fleece givers could be.

She wasn't going to let Joey, or anyone else, belittle the hurt or the struggles that she'd gone through just because she hadn't been the one jumped by a slimeball that afternoon. Yes, Val and Karl had been there for them both when they were needed, but, once again, it had been purely physical.

Joey had a man willing to wait, willing to romance her and become her friend before he became her lover. That was the biggest fantasy of all. And that was why it scared her friend.

The air whipped through Samair's hair as she pumped her legs and went higher and higher. She knew she'd forgive Joey for her outburst. She loved her, and that was what friends did.

She also knew that she would say good-bye to Val soon, because she wanted a man who was willing to romance her, to be her friend and her lover, and the only way she was going to get what she wanted was to hold out for it.

37

Samair slept on the love seat that night.

Joey was sound asleep in the bed when Samair got home from the playground, Mike lying right next to her but above the covers. The sight had made Samair's heart swell, and she was glad her friend had decided to smarten up.

After a restless sleep she woke up to Joey's make-up breakfast of bacon and eggs, with a side order of serious conversation.

"Mike's gone already," Joey said when she saw Samair's quick glance at the bathroom.

She reached out to pull the full plate in front of her and Joey's hand snaked out and covered hers. When their eyes met, Joey's green ones were bright with tears. "I'm sorry."

Samair turned her hand over to link their fingers. "I know you are, baby. It's okay."

"I don't know what got into me, Sammie. I was hurt, and it just made me want to hurt someone else so I wasn't alone. I didn't mean any of it."

"Yes, you did mean it. Maybe not all of it, but those things had to come from somewhere." She squeezed Joey's hand and smiled. "And it's okay. You're my soul sister, and I know you love me, just as I love you. That gives us permission to kick each other's ass every now and then."

A few sniffles and a hug, and they dug into their breakfast. "So, you're really going to give Mike a chance? No more temper tantrums if he makes you wait for the nookie?"

Color flooded Joey's cheeks and she turned to the fridge for more orange juice. "He's a good guy, and he was right. You were both right. I need to stop thinking that all I have to offer is my body."

A pang went through Samair. "It sounds like true love might really be happening here."

"Yeah," she nodded. "I'm going to let him romance me, and when we make love, it's really going to mean something."

Yay for her.

S amair was late. Again.

It was Tuesday afternoon and she was meeting Vera

for a late lunch. The morning had been a bit of a hectic one, to say the least.

Val had called to see how Joey was, and when Samair mentioned her lunch date there had been a tense silence. Then he'd just had two words. "Be careful."

Not knowing quite what to make of that, Samair had struggled with nerves over meeting with his ex-wife, and over what to wear. And when she saw the polished brunette looking sophisticated and beautiful in a simple gray silk sheath, she felt a bit overdressed.

Instead of going with something flowing and carefree, as had been her style of late, Samair had chosen to go with her own personal version of a businesswoman. A clingy electric blue pencil skirt with a slit up the middle and a plain white button-down blouse. And, of course, a matching electric blue bra that could be seen through the blouse.

Pushing aside her insecurities, Samair straightened her skirt, summoned her inner vixen, and strode up to the booth Vera occupied. "What a lovely restaurant, Vera. I've never been here before."

It was a bit out of her normal price range, but she figured it was Vera's invitation, Vera's bill.

"A family friend owns it and it's one of my favorites." She waved the waiter over and waited while Samair ordered her drink.

Samair fought the urge to order coffee, the grown-up

drink of choice, and stayed true to herself with a Diet Coke. They exchanged small talk and Samair relaxed. Vera was being charming and flirtatious, and it was fun.

After the waiter brought their meals, the subject of the Fetish and Fantasy show came up.

"It was a lovely show the other night," Vera said with a smile. "You're very talented."

A flush of pleasure mixed with pride. Samair had worked very hard, and it was nice to hear the praise from a virtual stranger. "Thank you. All I did was make the lingerie; Val did the rest."

" Yes, Valentine is a very . . . driven man."

For the first time Samair felt a tingle of unease over being with Val's ex-wife. The hair on the back of her neck stood up and her instincts perked up. She asked Vera what she hadn't been able to ask Val. "Is that what came between you two? His being driven?"

Her sleek eyebrows rose. "He hasn't told you?"

"We don't talk much when we're together."

"Ah yes, he's always been very lusty as well." Vera set down her fork and put her hands in her lap.

Samair sat straight and silent, waiting.

Finally Vera spoke. "Valentine's first and only true love is that club, and when he didn't spend a sufficient amount of time with me, I found other ways to amuse myself."

"You mean other men?"

"A married couple, actually. It was a mutually satisfying relationship for us, and when Valentine showed no interest in swinging, I selected another partner to take part with me. Valentine didn't like that, and he left me." She picked up her teacup and met Samair's gaze. "He still loves me, though, and I'm close to winning him back. I believe his affair with you makes him feel as if we're even."

"Even?" He'd left Vera because she'd had sex with someone else.

Pain knifed through her chest. If she'd needed confirmation that she was nothing more than a sexual partner to Val, that was it. He'd left his wife because he couldn't stand to share her, and he'd invited another man into bed with them.

"That's why I'm here, Samair. Valentine and I will be back together soon, and I'm not willing to share him anymore. I'd like you to leave him alone, and I'm willing to make it worth your while to do so."

Be careful.

Val's warning echoed in Samair's mind and her spine stiffened. "Worth my while?"

"Yes." Vera smiled, and for the first time Samair saw it as more predatory than seductive. "I think you have an amazing talent and I'd like to invest in your design label, on the condition that you stop chasing my husband."

Samair's mind raced. She fought through the emotions

swamping her to focus on what was right in front of her. Was this Val's way of making sure her one last fantasy came true at the same time he was cutting her loose?

Be. Careful.

She clasped her hands together under the table to still their trembling. "Invest how much?"

Victory shone in Vera's eyes as she described how she would set Samair up in a studio, set up accounts for her use at various wholesalers for fabrics and notions. She'd use her family name and connections to see that Samair got a chance to show her stuff to some industry friends in New York.

Basically, Vera offered her the sun, the moon, and the stars—if she would agree to stop seeing a man who only saw her as a sex partner anyway.

A man who she'd somehow come to care for, without even really knowing. No. She knew him. She knew he was strong, and safe, and sane. He was honest and straightforward. He was also a nice guy, despite the tall, dark, and dangerous thing he had going on.

She did know him, even if she didn't know his life story.

Shit, she'd spent four months getting to know Kevin before they'd even slept together, and they were together for almost two years before she caught him and Lisa together. She'd lived with Lisa for three years. Spending time together doesn't always mean you know someone. And she really did feel she knew Valentine Ward.

She knew him enough to trust him, even when he didn't tell her everything.

"It's an amazing offer, Vera. It truly is, and I'm so very thankful you think I'm talented enough to back me like that. But I'm afraid I'm not interested."

Vera's eyes narrowed and her lips pursed. "He won't stay with you. His nightclub means more to him than anything or anyone, and he'll give you up when I make him the same offer."

"That's okay." A weight lifted off her shoulders and she reached for her backpack. "I don't know what the future holds as far as Val and I are concerned. What I do know is that Trouble is mine, and it will remain all mine. If I've learned anything from the past, it's that I need to stay true to myself and my dreams, and being the sole power and inspiration behind Trouble is something I'm not willing to give up for anything."

She took all the money from her wallet and tossed it on the table as she stood to leave. She didn't want anything from Vera, not even lunch.

38

Val stewed all day, wondering what Vera was up to with Samair. That bitch of an ex-wife of his was out to hurt him, and that was fine, but if she fucked with Samair he would show her what true hurt was.

"Will you calm the fuck down, man?" Karl said. "My head hurts just watching you."

Val didn't slow his pacing. "If you don't like it, leave."

"Shit man, I'm sorry. I know how much this club means to you."

The club? He wasn't even thinking about the club. And that showed just how far gone he was. He was still short on the money to make the final loan payment; he had less than twenty-four hours, and no idea how to come up with it. And all he could think about was Samair.

As if his thoughts had conjured her, she was there. "We need to talk."

Karl stood and clapped him on the shoulder. "Call me if you need me, buddy."

When they were alone, Samair closed the door to his office and went to sit on the sofa. He watched her, every muscle in his body tense as she sat back and crossed her legs. She met his gaze and he could read nothing in her baby blues.

"Your ex-wife says you're getting back together."

"She's lying."

Her lips tilted in a soft smile. "I figured that one out for myself when she tried to buy me off in exchange for not seeing you again."

He leaned back against the edge of his desk and scrubbed a hand over his face, giving himself a moment to get his emotions under control. "That woman is amazing." Hungry for a hint to what was going on, he studied Samair's posture and her expression.

Val had never seen Samair look so closed off before. He wanted to ask what else Vera had said, but he couldn't. Instead he asked what she'd offered.

"Pretty much everything I could want. A studio to design in, accounts with suppliers, connections with the fashion industry."

Her gaze was intent on him as she rattled off the list, and a sour ball of disappointment settled in his gut. What irony that he was going to lose both the club and the woman who had reminded him there was more to life than work, at the same time, to the same woman.

After all, Samair had gotten everything she could want from him already. They'd covered the majority of sexual fantasies, with the exception of serious kink—which he didn't think she was interested in. Plus he'd helped her get her own business up and running. He really had nothing else to offer her.

"It sounds like a dream come true. I'm happy for you."

"I turned her down."

His breath caught in his throat. "You turned her down?"

"As much as all of her promises sounded like a dream come true, they took away the most important aspect of making Trouble exactly that."

Christ, she was killing him! Most women talked too much, but getting information out of Samair was worse than pulling teeth. "What's that?" he asked.

"If I let her do that for me, it wouldn't be mine," she said simply.

The sourness in his gut eased and relief loosened his tense muscles. All was not lost. "That's true. Vera likes to control everything, and everyone, she's involved with. I'm glad you turned down her offer."

"I turned it down because I want my business to be mine, not because of you." She stared at him. "In fact, all but two things have been crossed off my list of fantasies."

It hit him then that if he didn't start giving a bit more of himself, if he didn't take a chance and open up a little, she was going to walk away. And he still wasn't ready to let her go.

But, she'd said . . . "Two more things?"

The only way to get what she wanted wasn't to hold out for it. Instead, she was going to go after it.

She'd met Val because she hadn't been scared to let her inner bad girl out, to cause a little trouble, and that was how she was going to keep him.

She stood and sashayed closer, looking up at him from beneath her lashes. "Yes, two things." She put a hand on his forearm and urged him around the desk. "One of which is to have you sit in your chair and do absolutely nothing while I show you something."

With a gentle shove she had him in the high-backed leather chair behind his desk. Despite the heat that was creeping into his eyes as she eased up onto the desk in front of him, he looked quite . . . severe.

Almost principal-ish. It wasn't the clothes; he was still wearing his usual daytime outfit of jeans and a T-shirt, with his luscious locks loose about his face. It was his rigid posture, and the stern expression on that handsome face.

She wondered if he'd put her over his lap and paddle her for being bad.

Before her mind could go too far down that path she started to inch the hem of her skirt higher up her thighs. A surge of adrenaline went through her, her body heating, softening. This might be the last time she saw Val, and if it was, she wanted to be embedded into his memory forever.

Val sat in front of her, his hands curled lightly on his muscled thighs, his eyes steady as she reached up and undid the clip in her hair. She ran her hands through the fine strands and fluffed it. She wanted that "just out of bed" look that made his eyes gleam with hunger.

"Don't move," she warned. "Just watch."

Her hands drifted down her neck and brushed lightly over her breasts. She cupped them, thumbs rubbing over the nipples until they stood hard and proud through her clothing before her hands traveled down over her belly. She spread her thighs apart, lifting her skirt higher so he could see the tops of her stockings and the inches of bare flesh before her electric blue panties blocked his view of her dampening sex.

"Do you like what you see?"

"Very much." He met her gaze. "But I like it better when you're not wearing panties."

A thrill went through her. He always picked up on exactly what she wanted. "Your wish is my command," she said softly, and slipped her fingers up under her skirt to pull her panties down. She dropped them from her knees and hooked them on her foot. Straightening her leg, she waved them in front of Val. "For you."

He slipped them off her foot and lifted them to his face for a deep breath. Heat flooded her body and the intense rush of arousal made her sex clench.

Leaving her thighs spread so he could enjoy the view, she brought her hands back up and began to slowly unbutton her blouse. She watched Val's eyes flick back and forth from her hands and the skin she was slowly uncovering to her thighs and the skin that was already uncovered. Once all the buttons of her blouse were undone, she spread it off her shoulders so that it caught on her elbows. She arched her back and cupped her breasts through her bra. She lifted and squeezed and teased with Val's eyes glued to her movements.

He wanted that bra undone, it was clear in the way his hand started to reach out before his fingers curled and he stayed his movement.

"Good man," she murmured. "Don't touch, just watch."

One hand dropped to her thigh and began a leisurely walk toward her pussy. She could feel herself thicken as blood pooled between her thighs and she spread her thighs farther.

Λ naughty thrill filled her soul as she traced a fingertip over her swollen lips before slipping in between them to test the warmth and spread the juices.

With eyes closed, she let her mind go and began to pleasure herself. Her finger circled her swollen clit and the other hand pulled her breast out of the bra cup and began to tweak and pinch her nipple. She concentrated on the sensations rushing through her and the sound of Val's harsh breath as he watched her work herself toward orgasm.

As good as it felt, this was for him.

She spread her thighs even wider and bent her knees, tilting her pelvis and shoving a finger deep into her hole to fuck herself. Λ low groan reached her ears and she cracked her eyes open to see Val rubbing his cock through his pants.

"Stand up and take it out," she commanded.

He stood and, eyes glued to her hand, unzipped his jeans. Saliva pooled in her mouth when he pushed his jeans low on his hips and his cock jutted out into his hand. He stroked it slowly, the head gleaming purple, his hand visibly tightening when she licked her lips.

Feeling the heat of his eyes on her while she watched him made her blood run faster and her clit swell. The hard little nubbin was itchy and begging for more attention. She'd denied herself because she knew as soon as she focused on it again, she'd come quickly.

Not holding back, Samair pulled her wet finger out of her

hole. Slowly she brought her finger to her mouth, and when Val's eyes met hers, she licked it like a lollipop.

"Oh, baby," he growled and stepped forward.

"No!" she said sharply. "Stay there."

He froze in place, jaw clenched and nostrils flaring.

"Come with me. I want to watch you make yourself come." She placed her finger directly on her clit and began to flick it back and forth quickly.

When Val saw what she was doing, he gripped his cock, his strokes picking up the pace until he was pumping fast and hard. Their panting filled the room and she bit down on her bottom lip. The sight of him—hot, hard, and completely human as he put on a show for her—caused her heart to swell and tears to well in her eyes. He was beautiful.

Thighs spread as wide as could be, her skirt was pushed up around her hips and Val's eyes were locked on her fast-moving fingertip. Her breaths shortened, her belly tightened, and the room shifted as pleasure crashed through her in waves.

She cried out and welcomed the hot splash of Val's come on her bare skin as he threw back his head, his own guttural shout mixing with hers.

When she opened her eyes again, Val stood in front of her, watching her. Her chest tightened and she slid from the desktop and repaired her clothes. "That was number one. I wanted you to see all of me so you have something to visualize when you make your decision."

Straightening her spine, she stepped closer to him and cupped a hand over his cheek. The muscle in his jaw flexed beneath her touch and she tilted her head, locking eyes with him.

"The last fantasy on my list is you. All of you, with me, in more than just a string of sexcapades. I'm not going to say I love you, because I'm not sure I do. What I am sure of is that I feel more for you than I ever thought possible, and I'm not settling for less than everything you have to give." She kissed him softly, then spoke firmly. "Trust me, or let me go."

She stepped back, picked up her backpack, and gave him one last lingering look. He watched her, his eyes burning with unvoiced emotions, but said nothing.

Swallowing hard past the lump in her throat, she headed for the door. "You know where to find me."

39

"You sure you don't want her?"

Val tried to control his despair as he met Karl's gaze. "You know better than that," he growled. "Of course I don't want to give her up, but it's her or the club, and I've made the choice."

It wasn't the only choice he had to make, either.

Karl climbed onto Val's Harley, his baby, and started it up. Over the low rumble of the engine, Karl spoke clearly. "I know you love the bike, man, and the club means everything to you, but that long face is pitiful. If you want my opinion, you should chase down Samair and stake a claim. She's a good woman, and we both know those aren't easy to find."

Karl gave a small wave then took off. Val looked down at the check in his hand, made out to him from a lawyer buddy of Karl's who was willing to pay top dollar for the vintage 1955 bike. He hated to let go of her, but the check was just what he needed to make the final loan payment.

A look at his watch confirmed he had no time to waste. With a sigh he slid behind the wheel of his Camaro and headed for the bank.

Making the choice to sell the bike was easy compared to the one he still had to make.

Samair's ultimatum the day before had left his head spinning. His first instinct had been to let her walk away, but he knew that was pride. Ultimatums were ugly things and he hadn't liked it one bit. But he did understand it.

She was right. He'd given her every fantasy she'd mentioned; he'd given her pleasure, passion, and even playfulness. But he hadn't given her the trust that was needed to have a real relationship.

It wasn't easy, and not just because of Vera, either. He'd learned the hard way to only trust himself. Karl had pounded his way into Val's confidence, but it had taken time. He'd known Samair less than a month.

Yet the thought of never seeing her again made his stomach ache.

He pulled into the bank's parking lot and shut off his car.

Risqué was something that was completely his, and after today, no one could take it away. It was a goal that he'd been working toward all his life.

So why was the victory so hollow?

40

Samair waited for the rumbling thunder of a Harley coming down her street, but it never came. She tried sketching, she tried sewing, she even tried going over the orders from the show one more time, but she couldn't distract her mind from what she so desperately wanted to hear.

She hadn't expected him the night before. He had a club to run, and he probably needed time to consider what she'd said. But she'd been awake and tense since early morning, and she was going to crack soon.

It was time to accept that Valentine Ward had truly only been interested in a good time with her. The emotions, the connection between them . . . it had all been in her mind.

Tears welled and streaked down her cheeks and she finally gave in to the urge to cry.

No sooner had she thrown herself on the bed and buried her head in the pillow than the door buzzer rang. She almost ignored it, but a nagging in the back of her mind made her drag her ass from bed to answer the summons.

"Who is it?"

"Me."

Her heart kicked in her chest and her hand shook as she pressed the release to let him into the building. He was there.

She unlocked the door and made a quick dash into the bathroom. No way was she going to see him looking like hell. She splashed cold water over her face, ran a brush through her hair, and put some clear gloss on her lips.

It took less than three minutes and was the best she could do. When she opened the bathroom door, Val was standing in the middle of the small studio apartment. He had his leather jacket on, his hair down, and an unreadable expression on his face.

"Hi," she said.

His eyes softened, but he didn't say anything.

She went toward him, determined to stick to her guns, but unsure of exactly what to say. Oh, hell, she hated tiptoeing around. It just wasn't her style.

She dropped onto the love seat and patted the cushion

next to her. "Why don't you have a seat and stay a while. Tell me your life story," she said with a laugh.

Val's eyes widened, then his lips twitched and he sat down. "I don't know, that might take too long. How about I just hit some recent highlights—the ones that might convince you to take a chance on me?"

She struggled to breathe for a moment, then she nodded and smiled. "I'd like that."

Val met her gaze and spoke quietly. "I grew up pretty rough. My parents died when I was so young that I don't remember them; all I remember are the many, many foster homes I lived in. Most of them were good, but crowded. Some of them were hell. But the one thing they all had in common was that they were temporary. I always knew I'd have to move on, and things would change again."

He looked at her, gauging her reaction, and she smiled. She wanted to know this. She wanted to know everything. "Go on," she urged.

"When I was sixteen I skipped out on the system so I could look after myself. I worked odd jobs for money, but mostly I hustled pool. I was good at it, and I could live off what I made." He shrugged. "I spent so much time in bars that it was the only place I felt at home. Somehow, owning my own place became the dream. I worked hard, saved money, and when I hit thirty I had enough for a down payment on an empty warehouse. It took two more years of hustling and bartering, blood and sweat to turn that warehouse into Risqué, but I did it."

He paused, shaking his head as memories danced in his chocolate eyes. Samair remained quiet, scared that if she spoke and reminded him she was there, he'd stop.

"It didn't take long for the club to gather a regular crowd, and what I didn't know about running a nightclub, I learned fast. Sex and cheap drinks bring in the customers. Over the next year I kept improving the club, cleaning it up, making the drinks more expensive, bringing in cage dancers. I wanted it to be sexy but not sleazy, so it would draw a better crowd. And it did. When I met Vera, she was everything I thought I wanted. She was beautiful, sexy, sophisticated . . . and she wanted me." He met her gaze then. "At least, I thought she wanted me."

Somehow, she'd known Vera was behind it all. "What happened?"

He shrugged again. "I thought it was love. We got married, and because I refused to use any of her or her family's money or influence, I had to continue to work damn hard at the club. She didn't like being second place, as she saw it, and she thought that having an affair, and rubbing my face in it, would make me see things her way. Instead, it made me see things more clearly. So I left.

"I thought she'd be happy that I didn't want anything from her in the divorce. Karl wanted me to go after damages, but I just wanted out. I went into the marriage with nothing more than the club, and that was all I wanted when I left. Unfortunately, Vera took that as another insult. Our divorce was final just over a year ago, and three months ago she pulled some strings and had the bank call in my loan."

He explained to Samair how he needed one big event to raise a lump sum to pay off the loan by the fifteenth of the month—one day away—in order to keep the club.

"Did it work? Did the party bring in enough to keep the club?" No wonder he'd been so closed off. Ever since she met him, he'd been dealing not only with a childhood that would make it hard for anyone to give trust, but an ex-wife who was determined to make him pay for her mistakes.

Val shook his head. "Not entirely. The show brought in a lot of money, but not enough to clear the loan."

"Oh, Val!" Her stomach sank and she reached for him. Samair thought about everything he'd told her as she held his hand in both of hers. Then a thought hit her.

Had he just been using her?

He stared at her, as if he knew what she was debating in her mind.

Yes, she decided, he had used her.

But she'd been the one to seek him out; she'd also been the one to reiterate the fact that their relationship was strictly sexual when the emotions got too close to the surface. He'd played by the rules she'd set, and he also made sure that he was doing something good for her in return. He might've used her to bring money into the club for himself, but there was no denying that it had been good for her, too. She'd have never been able to do a launch for Trouble like that herself, and after everything else, he still hadn't made enough to keep his club.

"That sucks!" she said succinctly.

"It's all right." He smiled at her. "One of the lawyers in Karl's office has been drooling over my bike for months, so I sold it to him."

"You sold your Harley?"

"It was either that, or lose the club to Vera."

"Vera," Samair said. She chewed on her bottom lip and met Val's gaze.

"The bitch from hell who tried to take it all from me. Including you."

"You know, some might think it's not nice to call her a bitch from hell, no matter what she did."

"I call 'em like I see 'em."

She ducked her head and watched him from beneath her lashes. "And how do you see me?"

He reached out, gripped her hips, and pulled until she was flat on her back and he was stretched out over the top of her on the cramped love seat. His hands framed her face and he looked deep into her eyes. "I see you as mine for a long time to come."

Then he kissed her.

Epilogue

Samair jumped to her feet and let out a piercing rebel yell that echoed through the large auditorium. Val stood next to her with an indulgent grin in place as Samair clapped so hard her hands burned.

On stage in front of them, a spritely redhead took another bow with a man on each side of her. The curtain dropped, then raised again and the three took one last bow.

"She was amazing, don't you think?" Samair turned to Val, bursting with pride and pleasure for her friend.

"She was." He nodded. "And so were the costumes."

She elbowed him in the ribs.

Joey's debut performance with the newly formed dance troupe Outside the Box wasn't the only thing they were celebrating that night. After only four months, Trouble was operating in the black.

It helped that Val had a storage room at Risqué that they'd cleared out and turned into a small studio, and that since she lived with him now, she didn't have any rent to pay. Her parents still saw it as a hobby, not a business, and certainly not a career. But it didn't matter to her.

Brett understood, and even Cherish was coming around after getting a custom-made bustier-style gown for a Christmas gift. It wasn't until her sister wore the gown to a New Year's Eve party and saw everyone's envy that Cherish realized what she had, but that was okay, too. Samair had learned that everyone needed to learn things in their own time, and in their own way.

"Let's get going," she said to Val, who was already urging her toward the door.

"There's no hurry. Everything will be ready when we get there. You've terrorized my staff so much that they wouldn't dare mess this up. Besides that, we're all proud of her, too."

Val and the rest of the staff at Risqué were throwing Joey a surprise good-bye party in the private bachelor room under the stairs at the club. Samair knew that it would all be ready when they got there. That wasn't why she was in a hurry.

She threaded her arm into the crook of his and pressed

her breast against him. "Did I tell you I'm not wearing any panties?"

He looked down at her, his eyes darkening as amusement shifted to heat. "Really?"

"Really." She pressed closer and flashed him a promising smile. "And I've never had sex in a car before."